THE GARGOYLE'S GRACE

Doit

Octobre 23. 1811   Madame France
Madame France   soixante francs   260
passagi

Doit

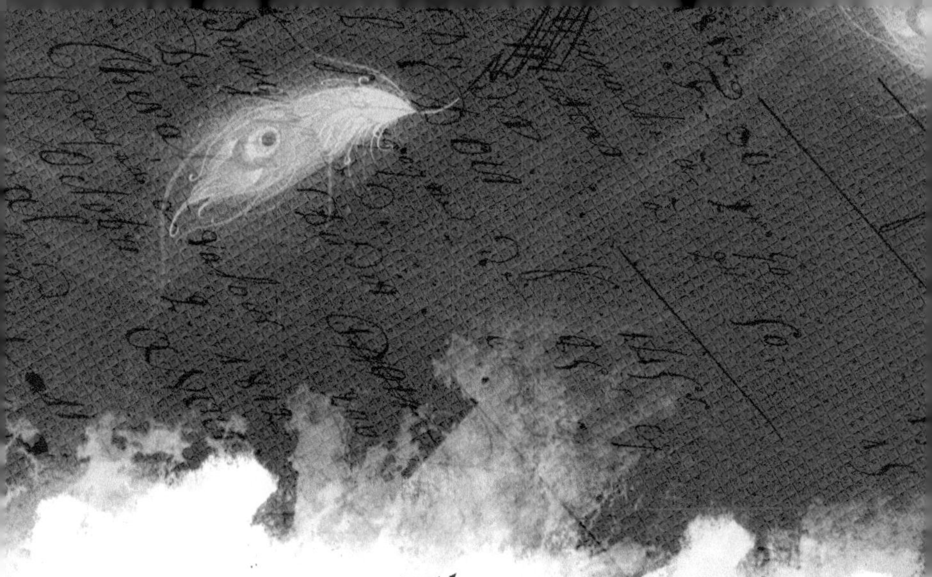

THE GARGOYLE'S GRACE

THE GARGOYLE KNIGHTS
BOOK ONE

L. ALEXANDER

The Gargoyle's Grace
The Gargoyle Knights Book One

ISBN: 978-1-958933-04-6 (Ebook)
ISBN: 978-1-958933-06-0 (Paperback)

Cover Design: Jessica, Enchanting Covers
Interior Design: Stephanie Anderson, Alt 19 Creative
Edited by: Krista Dapkey

*If Goliath and Elisa were one of your earliest OTP couples...
you're in the right place.*

*Especially if you ever pretended you were Elisa,
running with Goliath a great shadow flying above you...
protecting you... chasing you.*

And you wanted to be caught.

*Demona was a fool.
Gorgeous, but a fool all the same.*

MY DARLING,
you will never be
UNLOVED BY ME,
you are too well
TANGLED IN MY SOUL.
— F. SCOTT FITZGERALD

AUTHOR'S NOTE

This novella is suggested to be read after *The Demon's Deal*, The Demon Princes Book 1. While this story can be consumed on its own, there is quite a bit of context around this world, the characters in it and the situations that take place in this story that are explained there.

While this is not a dark romance, there are some potentially triggering themes that come up throughout the book. You can find a list of tropes and content warnings below.

Please reach out to me directly for specifics if needed, I'm more than happy to give details, page numbers—whatever helps you best decide if your wellbeing and this story are compatible.

Tropes: soul mates, who hurt you, revenge, gargoyles and demons, pseudo-medieval European setting, praise, affection through sarcasm & care-giving, Ms. I'm fine, I can do it myself meets Mr. sit down & let me help you, later in life second true love romance

Content: explicit violence and brief gore, explicit sexual content (including themes of primal play, size difference, edging, just one more, etc.), mention of previous drugging & kidnapping, discussion of infertility

THE RIGHT SIDE of my face throbbed angrily as I blinked back to consciousness. It took several attempts to shake the drowsiness weighing me down and clear my vision.

Aches and pains all over my body let themselves be known as I forced movement into my heavy limbs. My head swam as I pulled myself to a sitting position, and a groan croaked out of my throat, echoing off the bare walls. The absence of a response to the noise gave me hope I was alone—for how long was anyone's guess, but I didn't intend on wasting any time leaving while I could.

The floor I'd been sprawled upon was nothing more than packed dirt. Light streamed in through dirty, cracked windows hung more than halfway up the massive walls. The ceiling was a ridiculous distance away, its heavy beams strung with cobwebs so thick I could have fashioned a sweater from them. Whitewash peeled from the wall's wide blocks in several old layers, and there was a musty smell that wouldn't clear from my nose.

As I looked around, searching for a door, I trudged backwards through my memories until the truth about what happened rose up, harsh and ugly. My mistress, Calla, and I had been at the beer garden, sharing a friendly meal. She didn't get out much, and I'd been left in charge of showing her around the city while her mate and my boss, Rylan, took care of an errand.

We'd spent quite a lovely day visiting the market and some shops. Lunch at the beer garden seemed like a lovely way to relax at the end of that. Instead, it had been a terrible mistake. One I might never forgive myself for.

While we'd sat there talking, eating our sausages and enjoying the breeze, someone had drugged our ale. My faculties had left me, and I was forced to watch as she was taken away, unable to do anything to help her.

Then, three men had bundled me off between them. None too gently, they'd carried me to a cart, pulled a sack over my head, and tossed me in. I tried to keep track of the turns we took after leaving the beer garden, but the drug had made me slow, confused. By the time we arrived at the warehouse, I didn't have the first clue where I'd ended up.

I'd been left there—wherever *there* was—to sleep it off after the men pushed me around between them, laughing as they treated me like worthless cargo. Unable to move, speak, or fight, I'd scraped the whole right side of my face against some kind of equipment as I'd fallen, then my body bounced off of wood and metal, collecting bruises and cuts.

Anger burned hot in my chest at the recollection. Using the block wall to help me, I carefully pressed myself to my feet. My legs were wobbly, and my stomach revolted at the motion, but couldn't allow myself to stop moving. I slid along the wall, chunks of paint breaking off under the weight of my hand. Sweat coated my brow, and every inhale burned as I tried to fill my lungs.

It took several long minutes to cross the length of the sparsely filled room. I paused at the door, listening for any activity over the thump of my heartbeat in my ears. Breath sawed roughly in and out of my chest as I willed strength into my limbs. It was still quiet, which left me equal parts hopeful and terrified.

Pushing the door open slowly, I crept forward, straining to hear any bit of movement beyond my own breath and the rustle of my dress against the rough wall. When there was no resistance, no yelling or indication of life at all outside of my own ... I ran. It was ungainly, as my steps were halting and unsure while I shook off the remainder of the drugged ale left within me. I hadn't had cause to run in more than a decade, either, so my body protested the motion and every step as I went.

Using the observatory tower at d'Arcan—the collegium where I worked as head cook—as a compass point, I fumbled my way through the city in the early morning light. Glad to slow from a run to a hasty trot, I passed into the densely populated city center. My muscles ached as I forced them to continue moving, keeping my head down so the passersby weren't alerted to the sorry state I was in.

As I turned down a side alley in a familiar neighborhood, I realized I hadn't kept track of where I'd come from. I'd not easily find the warehouse again. Frustrated that I'd been in such a hurry, I swore aloud, garnering a harsh look from one of the maids hanging fresh wash.

I apologized and found the words a slurred mess as they crossed my lips. She shook her head and turned away, no doubt writing me off as a morning-after drunken holdover. I wasn't sure if my memory and mouth were slow because of the drug or something else, but I hated it.

Chest burning, I made my way around apartment blocks, through side streets and alleys not traveled well on my way back to my workplace. My home. Dread settled deep in my bones as I went over the events of the last day in my mind.

By the time the Collegium d'Arcan was within reach, every part of my body screamed at me. The iron gate clanged into its latch as I entered the courtyard, echoing through my chest in a solid, comforting way. As I crossed the cobblestones, considering possible ways to get in touch with the archmage and looking forward to washing the shame from my skin, my legs gave out. I slid to my knees, overwhelmed by the relief of being somewhere safe. Shame slithered down my neck right after, the crushing weight of my failure stirring an uncomfortable storm of emotions inside my chest.

My head snapped up as the doors to the main building crashed open. One large man I knew, along with one I didn't, came through, stress clear in their features. "Magnus?"

"Grace! What's happened to you?"

"Is Rylan with you?"

"Yes, he's inside. You're hurt—" The fire in his eyes was flattering, but I didn't have time to consider it at the moment.

"I'll be alright. I need to speak with Rylan, it's urgent."

"Of course." He nodded tightly and reached out to help me up.

Unsteady, I got to my feet again, and with Magnus's help, was able to make it inside. The fair man hanging quietly off to the side seemed oddly familiar, though I was certain I'd never met him before. When Magnus left me at the worn dining room table, I was supplied with coffee and a healthy dollop of whiskey, then my young helpers bustled this way and that as the men tromped around angrily. I tried to brace myself as well as I could and planned my words.

"What's happened?" Rylan asked, coming across the room with electricity streaming from him, panic in his eyes.

My helpers scattered back to the kitchen, and I didn't blame them. He was imposing and could be terrifying when he was riled, even if he didn't mean to be.

"I'm a fool, is what happened," I admitted.

"Where's Calla?" he asked.

"I don't know." I dropped my eyes to the table, too ashamed to look him in the eye.

"You don't ..."

Magnus stepped between us. "*Settle*, demon. She is not your enemy."

I appreciated that he'd protect me, but if the archmage wanted to hurt me, I'd earned it.

"I would never hurt Grace," Rylan tried to assure us both.

"Who's done this to you?" Magnus grunted, pacing irritably. His fists clenched at his sides.

"I'm alright," I insisted, though I desperately wanted some healing tea and a hot bath to soothe my aches away.

"You're not. There's blood on your dress, and these cuts on your face need tending to," Rylan agreed.

"Shall I fetch your kit?" the fair man offered.

Rylan gave some instructions for where to find it, and he left swiftly, still managing to look regal even as he moved with purpose.

"Tell me what happened, Grace," Rylan demanded, taking a seat next to me.

"I've failed you both," I sobbed, unable to keep my desperate shame inside any longer.

"Come now. I very much doubt that, Grace. Start at the beginning."

I gulped at the coffee in my mug, the whiskey in it burning away the last of the musty odor that clung to my nose. Then I did what he asked and told him as much as I could remember while he treated my wounds. I refused his magic—the scars I'd earned from the altercation were mine to bear. They'd be a reminder of how badly I'd fumbled one of the most important tasks I'd ever been given.

I had faith that Rylan would find his mate, and clung to that as part of my own salvation for such a mistake.

Just like I would find the men who'd done this to me, and make sure they paid for their part in things.

CHAPTER 1
GRACE

"I'll be out for the evening," I instructed Sara, my current kitchen helper. I gathered up the food I'd prepared to take with me to my parents' apartment and stowed them in a large handled basket to carry with me. "Once the dishes are done, you're excused."

"Yes, Miss Grace."

"Good girl." I spun and Sara trailed behind me as I left the kitchen proper and went out into the dining room. I turned to her; the delicate little thing's eyes wide as she trotted at my side. "And if the headmaster needs anything—"

"He can very well get it himself."

"Archmage!" I stopped in my tracks, my boss smiling at me as he approached. "Did you need something before I go?"

He bowed his head in greeting, and Sara, even more wide-eyed than before, took him in. It didn't help that his friend Magnus, a mountain of a man even larger than my employer, was a few steps behind him. I understood her nervousness, but they were both a soft touch. The archmage might appear large and intimidating but was the kindest boss one could hope to ever have. He was also a literal demon, but I'd learned firsthand since coming to this school that the most-feared creatures were often highly misunderstood. The same extended to Magnus who was one of the stone kin—a gargoyle, to be precise.

"You go on to your dinner, Grace. I can manage my way around the kitchen. Calla and I are just a bit peckish this evening, and you know how *he* is." His kind amber eyes shifted from my face to the girl beside me as he gestured over his shoulder at Magnus. Rylan gave a playful wink, and Sara smiled, enjoying being in on the joke. "Besides, I'm sure Sara can help if there's something I can't find."

"That's quite rude," Magnus grumbled, but he was smiling. "By now I'm sure Grace has skillfully managed to accommodate for my needs. She's an expert, or so I'm told."

"Too true," I said, genuinely flattered by the compliment despite the fact that *I'd* been the one to tell him that ... repeatedly.

Magnus's appetite was truly immense and had become quite the running joke. My irritation over having to adjust for his intake when he wasn't consistent about being on the grounds to feed was, however, quite real. Mostly.

"In any case, I'm sure I can find what we need with Sara's help, of course."

The girl hastily nodded, clearly still slightly petrified by the idea of being solely responsible for their snacks. Usually, at least one of her three sisters would also be in the kitchen with us, but they'd been pulled away for other duties around the collegium.

I resisted the urge to reach up and touch the shiny ridges on my cheek. My shoulders had tensed at the mention of the archmage's wife's name, but I shifted to disguise it. "Very well. Sara?"

"Ma'am?"

"Don't let that one"—I pointed at Magnus—"take more than two servings. I don't have deliveries coming for a few days yet."

Rylan chuckled, and Magnus raised a hand to his chest as though wounded. "I take more abuse in this room than anywhere else in my life, and I'm a *soldier*. You're brutal, woman."

I raised my eyebrow at his commentary, shaking my head as his mouth slid into a grin. "You know the solution to that, of course," I prompted.

"Which is?"

"Stop coming into this room."

His eyes and mouth went wide, and Rylan laughed openly, amused as always, by our trading barbs. "Surely you don't mean that."

I arched an eyebrow in response, which had him grumbling under his breath while Rylan laughed harder. He did offer some comfort after a moment with a brief shoulder pat.

"You have this in hand, Sara?"

"Yes ma'am," she confirmed with a confident nod, and the trio went into the kitchen together.

I inhaled and set off through the hall, arm already aching from the weight of the basket. Once out in the early evening air, I finally felt able to take a full breath. I hated that I still felt so uncomfortable around the people I considered close as family. But I'd failed them in an unforgivable way, and atoning was a process I'd just begun to work through.

As I strode out of the gate and into the city streets, the organized chaos of industry humming around me lightened my mood. The further I got from my place of employment, the easier I was able to pretend that everything was okay. I was simply a woman headed to have dinner with her parents. Just another day in an ordinary life.

Except that it wasn't. It was the end of the month, and that meant after dinner I'd have another errand to run, one that I looked forward to less and less.

"Evening, Grace! Care for a stem or two this week?"

"You know I can't resist you, Maurice." I hated to part with even a single coin, but the aged little florist had a big piece of my heart. He'd run the same cart on the same corner since I was a little girl.

I handed over the money, and he pulled out a small bouquet I knew he'd made up special for me.

"My mother will thank you as well," I said, tucking the paper-wrapped bundle under my arm.

"Give her my best!" He gave a stiff bow, bending at the waist with his arm across his chest.

I waved, wishing there would never come a day where I didn't find him behind his cart. I knew it was likely he'd be retired soon, though. I secured the basket as close to my body as I could and maneuvered through crowded alleys where food vendors slung their tasty wares and around avenues where foot traffic slowed us all down to barely moving.

The sun was on its final descent as I finally made it to the little apartment block where my parents lived. Expecting me, they didn't even have their front door closed.

"What's this?" I asked, walking in and setting the basket down on the small slab of countertop that separated the kitchen from the living area. "Anyone could stroll in and take what they wanted."

My father laughed, planted both hands on the armrests, and lifted himself from his well-loved chair. "Not much to take, but if they did any such thing, then they probably need it more than we do."

His generosity was one of the things I loved most about him, despite the trouble it had gotten him into. "I brought your favorite," I said, allowing him to lean in and kiss my scarred cheek as I unloaded the basket's contents and gathered up plates. "And some of that ointment you like."

"You're too good to me, Gigi."

I shook my head. Every time he used my childhood nickname, I felt decades younger. "I brought these for Mama too. Where is she?"

My dad cleared his throat as he fished around in a cabinet for a vase. "She'll be home later."

"Later?" I asked, worried by that answer. "How much later?"

He filled a milky white glass container with water and put the flowers into it. "I'm sure she'll be here before you have to go." He fidgeted with the bouquet, avoiding my eye.

"Papa." I pinned him with a look as I handed over a plate full of his favorite casserole, and he folded.

"She took another child-minding job this week," he said, eyes guilty.

"How many is that now?" I filled my own plate, and we took them to their small dining table.

"Six." He grimaced as though the word tasted bad. I knew he felt terrible that she was having to do such things.

I put my hand over his gnarled one as he tried to pick up his fork and failed … several times. "It'll work out," I promised.

He blinked at me as though working out what he wanted to say, but finally just nodded while transferring his fork to his other hand. We ate in silence for a few minutes, the shouting of children from the yard outside and of neighbors calling one another for their own evening meals filtered through the open door.

"So, how are your girls shaping up?" he asked, knowing it would cheer me to talk about the new additions at the collegium.

Well, somewhat new. They'd been brought on several months ago now, but they'd been one of the best things to happen to d'Arcan as far as I was concerned.

"Wonderful. Little Sara is proving to be quite the baker. In fact, she's the one who made your dessert. And Bridget loves to wash clothes, so you can only imagine how thrilled we all are to let her scrub and rinse to her heart's content."

He frowned between bites. I was glad to see him eating enthusiastically. He'd lost several pounds recently, which was one of the reasons I'd begun bringing dinner with me during my weekly visit. Mama being out at odd jobs until unpredictable times certainly was another decent excuse. But I truly did show my love through food, and this was one of the ways I could give them a bit of the best of me.

"An odd passion, that," he said, eyebrows up. "Doing the washing. Who would have thought?"

I laughed. I suspected it had something to do with the fact that they'd never had more to their names than a single dress at a time, but that was just a guess.

"To be sure, it's strange, but certainly nobody's going to argue with her. They're such good kids."

"Most of them are," he said with a wink. "Even the ones with a bit of vinegar in their veins." I batted my eyelashes innocently, making him laugh at my denial of having been such a child.

We got all the way through our slices of the lemon custard pie Sara had baked before Mama finally came through the door.

"Oh, my girl!" she gushed, holding my face in her palms as she dipped down to kiss my forehead. "I'm so sorry I'm late."

"I'll make you a plate," I offered as she sank gratefully into my vacated chair.

"Thank you, my darling. What a day." She smoothed back several wild hairs that had escaped her gray-and-white braid. "Those younglings gave me a run for my money. I'm not as agile as I used to be, and I'm certain the ones I was sent to look after are mostly feral. This looks delicious!"

I squeezed into the third chair, the one wedged next to the wall with a crooked leg. As Mama enjoyed her food, I allowed myself to sink into the spirited after-work discussion with my parents. We had very few moments like that between us anymore, and I didn't want to ruin it by mentioning the elephant in the corner of the room that wouldn't go away.

"The flowers are lovely today. How is Maurice?"

"He seemed well." I picked up the empty plates before either of them could move to and got them washed just as quickly. My innate sense about when people were ready for food or for dishes to be retrieved was one of my points of pride.

I tucked the leftovers into their small ice box and allowed my mother to slip a coin pouch into my pocket when my father wasn't looking. We settled into the living room, talking about how their week had been, how the girls at the collegium were coming along, anything to keep us all distracted.

Too soon, the sun was fully down, and the chill of the evening floated through the open front door. It was time for me to leave. With lingering hugs and plenty of worry to go around, I put on a brave smile and braced myself for what came next.

CHAPTER 2
MAGNUS

I F ANYONE EVER wanted to torture me, all they'd have to do is leave me tied to a chair in the mystical council's chambers for a week. I'd find a way to meet my own demise one way or another if forced to endure the insufferable meetings any longer than I already did.

My position as liaison was useful in many ways, but the endless discussions between men who never went out in the field to see or do the things they were making decisions about drove me to madness. Each and every one of them loved to hear themselves speak and took every opportunity to do so. It was especially bad during these mixed council meetings where multiple factions of creatures were represented. It was bad enough when it was just the stone kin, but adding in the mages made everything move slower because everyone wanted to be in charge.

"Have you anything to report, General Aurichal?"

I straightened, shaking off the doze I had fallen into at the sound of my name. I stood and approached the long bench of officials, an assortment of men and women representing each group, seven for each.

"General Magnus Aurichal, reporting for the gargoyle contingent," the scribe said, stepping forward to announce me to the room. The formality was always strangely embarrassing.

"Nothing new in regards to the missing, unfortunately, though I continue to follow any lead that is presented."

"Noted. Next—"

"Apologies, council, but I must advise that there seems to be an influx of crime in the city. Enough to warrant concern. More shipments are being pilfered before they reach their destination, violence is erupting in the street over minor infractions—"

"Yes, all duly noted, General. The unrest of the humans is not unexpected, and they have their own methods for policing things." The councilman waved his hand as though such things were inconsequential.

"Of course." I frowned, but proceeded. "Also, the lower-level demon horde outbreaks are increasing in frequency, though overall volume and strength has diminished. Myself, Archmage Stolas, and other stone kin have been successful at putting them down thus far, but the way they are concentrating around Revalia is unusual."

"Thank you for your report, General. Your concerns are all noted and will be monitored. Maintain your patrols. There's no dispensation for additional man power at this time. Do you have any other concerns?"

Not aside from the significant ones I just listed that you have no interest in, I thought grumpily. Instead of saying as much, I simply shook my head. "No, sir." I gritted my teeth while giving the honorific. The more I dealt with these people, the less I believed they had any interest in what actually happened beyond these hallowed halls and their own posturing.

"Your assignment remains the same and will continue until we see further progress. Patrol routes and staffing are at your discretion, but please remind all stone kin that they are to be vigilant and above all, remain *unseen*." He looked at me over the top of his ridiculous little half-moon spectacles, impressing the importance of this upon me as though it weren't something even little fledglings just learning how to use their wings were taught. "You're to return next month as scheduled for briefing. Excused."

He called on the next poor bastard before I even had a chance to move. Stunned, I gave a polite nod before backing away. As I glanced over, I spotted General Gaius Caledon, who was pointedly looking away from me and toward the council bench. No matter. We weren't friends, but I wouldn't have called us enemies either. We did the same job, though in a very different way much of the time.

Once clear of the attendee benches, I turned and strode quickly out of the chamber. As I made my way down the wide marble-floored hall, I inhaled, breathing easier now that I was out of that stuffy room full of bureaucrats.

I thought I'd been pressing my luck double-booking my evening, but thankfully, the council had released me instead of wanting to pick apart every inch of my progress where several assignments were concerned. I wasn't sure which option I preferred.

I walked instead of using my wings as I wound my way into the center of the city. The sun was still not fully set, and the humans gathered too densely for me to travel the way I preferred. My contact, Will, worked evenings at the smithy in order to catch the cool breeze while toiling over the forge. He saw much, worked with many, and always had good information to share.

I stopped at the cart selling grilled meat skewers and bought two for each of us. While mostly a kindness, I also understood too well that information flowed better on a full stomach or with much wine.

The rhythmic *clang* of the hammer meeting the anvil could be heard a full block away. I always wondered how the neighbors felt about his preferred evening shift. I'd bet none of them would be brave enough to mention it in any case. If you were smart, you didn't complain to the man surrounded by fire and swords that he was making too much noise.

"You're early," he muttered as I walked into the shop. He had a long blade carefully balanced in his tongs as he moved toward a wide water trough.

"I come bearing gifts," I said, waving the skewers.

"One I'll gladly accept." Will nearly groaned in appreciation as he sniffed the fragrant air. "This blade has given me no end of trouble today, so I've not stopped to eat." The metal sizzled as it touched the cool water, and steam rose in a billowing cloud above the bath.

He shed his heavy leather gloves, tucking them under his arm as he reached out for the food. "Be well," he said by way of blessing, then enthusiastically tore into the meat with his teeth.

"And you," I replied, following his lead.

"I don't have much for you today," Will said over his mouthful, shaking his head as though admitting such was a disappointment to him. "Just more talk from the merchants that loads are arriving light—like missing *cases* of goods. The food vendors seem particularly upset." He chucked the first bare stick into the flames of his fire. "But most understand that when people are hungry, they do desperate things."

Indeed. I had several things on my list to discuss with the city council, which unfortunately was a whole separate entity from the magical councils I already met with. With Rylan away, it would be a while until that could happen, but that only gave me more time to gather evidence for my proposals.

"Any new contraband popping up?"

He shook his head, chewing a massive bite. "No. Your cleanup efforts a while back seem to have disrupted the whole business."

I grunted, pleased. Magical contraband—black market potions, spells, charms, and the like—had been flowing into the city for several months. Non-approved practitioners had been selling them, and untrained laymen had been using them. Several people had ended up dead because of it. Thankfully, we'd rooted out the issue, though not without cost. The people who had kidnapped the archmage's wife were the ones found responsible for both creation and distribution.

It was to my great pleasure that they were all dead now.

Will took a deep drink from a waterskin and gestured to the open archways that served as doors. "Shall we take a breath of clean air? I could use some cooling off." Sweat dotted his smudged forehead and there were rings of salt on his clothing.

"Of course."

I followed him into the grassy courtyard where he gave me a quick inventory of the weapons he'd been hired to make since I'd last seen him. Nothing felt out of the ordinary, but it was often hard to tell until it was too late when it came to things like swords and daggers.

"As always, I appreciate your help, Will." I put my hand in my pocket, palming a decent-sized coin. I shook his sooty, rough hand, making the transfer.

"My pleasure, Magnus. Anything you'd like me to keep my eye on this next little while?"

"Nothing new. Of course, if you see anything of interest before I'm scheduled to come by, just send me a message at the guild hall."

He nodded. "You sure I can't interest you in a blade?"

It was a long-running joke between us, as he naturally thought his craftsmanship at the very least equal to that of my kin, if not superior. "Not today," I replied, as I always did.

"Maybe another time then." He chuckled and headed over to the small well. Drawing a bucket of water, he then used it to clean his blackened hands and face.

"Perhaps." I didn't have the heart to tell him I would likely never carry a weapon forged by anything other than stone kin hands. He was a gifted artist at his craft, but his items were not meant for me. I gazed across the road, stunned to find a familiar face among the crowds moving through the square. "See you soon, Will."

"Aye," he grunted, already on his way back inside to continue his battle with the sword that was giving him so much trouble.

I frowned as I made my way across the street. I couldn't think of anyone I'd expected to see less in this part of town, at this time of night. Though she looked as though she was thinking the exact same thing of me the closer I got.

This would certainly be interesting.

CHAPTER 3
GRACE

I PULLED MY HOOD up over my hair, taking care to not let the heavy iron gate slam behind me as I exited the courtyard of my parents' apartment block.

The bustle of business in the city had slowed way down from just a few hours prior. Families were gathered for their evening meals, the scent of onions and meat in the air as business was put to rest until sunrise.

Well ... most business.

As the sun dropped fully below the horizon, a chilly breeze teased at my face and hands. Thanks to our weekly dinner, my stomach and heart were full, though quite unsettled.

My heart galloped behind my ribs as I stepped along the packed dirt avenue, leaving the well-lit residential area behind. I slipped a hand into my skirt pocket, nervously checking the weight of the leather pouch inside.

The payment was short this month.

And it wasn't the first time.

I mentally rehearsed the little speech I might have to give about why we were behind. Father's palsy was acting up thanks to the chill in the air and mother had lost several of her laundry clients due to having to care for him but was doing her best to replace them.

Last month I'd sacrificed my necklace as collateral to make up the difference. Despite my protests, my mother had given me her wedding ring, just in case. It would join my necklace this month. If next month wasn't better, I wasn't sure what else we'd have left to give.

Shaking the negative thought away, I turned into the alley where the broker had a storefront under a weathered apartment. The small food market on the corner was already shuttered for the evening, and the residents lingering outside watched me silently as I passed them by.

All too soon, I was standing outside the scarred yellow door, inhaling an acrid breath for courage, I rapped my knuckles on the wood in the pattern I'd been given at my last visit. I'd get a new one tonight, as well.

As the door creaked open just enough for a face to be seen, the massive form of one of Lawrence Caster's henchmen was revealed. "State your business," he growled.

"I'm making a payment," I responded, straightening my shoulders. I reminded myself that these were just men and I could handle myself. Lawrence was a man, at least. His hired muscle were all part stone kin. But I had something they wanted. It would be fine. At least that's what I kept telling myself to keep the panic shoved down.

The door opened wide, and I pushed past the man, heading for the side room where Lawrence conducted business.

"Right on time, Miss Jardin." Lawrence Caster's cragged face turned from me to the man taking up all the space on a small love seat at the side of the room. It was not the first time I'd seen him here, and I couldn't help but wonder what his role was with this loan shark.

"Gaius." I tipped my head in greeting.

"Grace." He gave me a lopsided grin along with a lingering stare. Both sent chills skittering down my spine. My adrenaline surged; my body recognized the danger in his interest—just as it had the last time we'd met.

Large like Magnus, but in many ways much more feline, Gaius reeked of predatory intent. Tall and broad, his features were all sharp angles and severe lines, even in his human form. As a gargoyle, he was one of the most intimidating creatures I'd ever come across.

His arm brushed mine as he left the room, and I struggled to keep my expression neutral. I was sure he could smell the fear pouring off me, but there was no helping it. I was also quite sure he'd done it on purpose because he enjoyed provoking such a reaction.

"Let's have it then." The broker reached out a weathered hand to me, and I withdrew the pouch from my pocket. He dumped the contents onto his desk, sorting through the coins with his fingertips.

"My father's condition has been worse lately, but we're doing everything we can to make up the difference—"

"You're half a measure light, Miss Jardin. Again." His cold gaze met mine, a question in them.

"My mother has offered her wedding ring as a gesture of good faith." I slipped the golden band down my finger, fighting the urge to clench my fist every step of the way.

"Appreciated," he said, his eyes never leaving mine as I set the jewelry in his palm. "You understand what happens if this continues." His tone communicated an unspoken threat.

"We do. We'll be back on track next month."

He said nothing as he leaned to the side and dropped my mother's ring in a locked case inside one of his desk drawers. I couldn't help but wonder how many family heirlooms he had in there, all stacked together without reverence or care. How many lives he'd ruined after promising aid.

"We appreciate your generosity and patience," I recited, knowing that flattery would only get me so far but also that at least a little was expected. "My father has always spoken highly of you and your support of his business. He wouldn't have been successful all those years without you." Bile rose in my throat at the lie in those words. My mother and I should have known better, seen the debt growing. The lengths he went to in order to keep paying, even when it destroyed his body, his hands.

"It is my history with your father that has allowed me to extend some ... flexibility to your family over this loan." He steepled his fingers together, looking somber. "The balance is not negligible but could very well be paid off within the year. However, my patience is running very thin. Nobody else would get such kindness if they were repeatedly short. Do you understand?"

My hands grew clammy, and my heart slammed against my ribs. I knew the warning in his words was not exaggerated. All the bravado I'd worked up earlier vanished under his cold stare.

"Yes sir."

"Good. I will not accept any more jewelry in trade. I do not have a need for gold or jewels. I need *coin*." He bent his head and grabbed a quill to mark this month off in his ledger. The number of marks, the years of payments, the way the debt grew despite the effort to pay it down because of his exorbitant interest rate ... it all sickened me.

"If you cannot make the full payment next month, we will come to an ... alternative arrangement."

My breath stalled in my throat. "What kind of arrangement?" I asked, voice steady but higher than I'd have liked. I wanted nothing more than to be out from under this man's thumb, but there were some lengths I refused to go to.

"One of my men has expressed willingness to pay off the balance for you."

I went over the words in my head, not quite understanding. Lawrence stared back at me as I opened and closed my mouth several times, words failing me. "I'm sorry, I don't understand. Why would they do that?"

He chuckled, the sound dry and hollow. "Let me say that again. He'd be willing to pay off the balance. For *you*."

"I ..." My heart landed in my throat, twisting my gut. My dinner threatened to rise. I knew without asking that it was Gaius. It had to be. The spot on my arm he'd brushed against began to itch, even through two layers of clothing.

He'd been posted at the collegium more than once since I'd started working there, though never when Magnus was around. I made sure to keep my distance, though I offered him the same kindness I did everyone else who came through—partly because it was my job and partly because of their connection to the archmage. His interest had not gone unnoticed, though I'd done my best to shut down any conversation that veered away from polite or professional.

"Our business here is done." He closed the ledger with a snap and waved me off after tapping out the new code knock on the cover.

"Thank you for your understanding." I gave an awkward half bow as I left and avoided meeting the eye of the men sitting in the strange living room, but my skin crawled under their gaze anyway.

"See you around, Grace," Gaius drawled.

Despite better judgment, I looked at him as I pulled open the door. I forced a small smile and walked out, hoping to lose the slimy feeling that always clung to me after going into that building.

My steps were quick as I headed back the way I'd come.

All along the dimly lit street, adults gathered in small clusters, enjoying an evening drink while children played nearby, getting the last of their leisure time in before bedtime.

I stopped to hand a weathered ball made from leather scraps back to a little boy, and he said, "Thanks, lady," before scurrying off back to his friends. I found myself smiling, remembering something my mother had told me at least a thousand times. *Even in the darkest of places, where the desperate go to find help, there's light.*

She was rarely wrong.

We'd been that light for the children in our neighborhood for years and years. Dad's butcher shop fed the hungry, and Mom's restless hands kept them busy, clothed, and often, educated. They deserved to be free of this burden once and for all.

I was just past the market when I came to a stunned stop.

Magnus was across the square at the blacksmith. As I watched, he dipped a hand into his pocket, then shook the man's hand. There was no way for me to prove it, especially with the size of his palm, but he'd almost certainly just passed along a coin. As though he felt me staring, Magnus looked up, just as surprised to see me as I was to see him.

Frowning, he crossed the distance between us. "Grace? What are you doing clear out here?"

"I could ask you the same," I said, deflecting.

He scanned the area, pausing as he looked down the street I'd come from. "I have business out this way."

"As do I." My words were clipped, my nerves displaying outwardly as anger.

His nostrils flared and he pressed heavy fingertips into my lower back, guiding me toward the center of town. It was then I realized my mistake. "You have people nearby, yes? But that's not where you were."

"I had dinner with my parents this evening," I said, forced to take two steps for every one of his. It suddenly occurred to me that I'd left the basket behind at their apartment, not to mention my favorite pie plate.

"And then what did you do?" he asked, the grumble in his voice irritating. As if he had any right to ask me such things. To know what I did in my own time.

"What were *you* up to, exchanging coin with that smithy?" I asked, turning my head so I could glare at him.

"Paying for services rendered," he said simply, as though that were the most obvious thing in the world.

"Oh? What are you having made? I'd love to see it. I thought you had your own guild for weapons and such."

"We do."

I shook my head, angling toward one of the streets that would take us a more direct route. "You keep your secrets then, and I'll keep mine."

We walked in silence past the neat rows of tall, connected houses. The set of his jaw and tense breathing told me he was waiting for me to start talking. He was in for several surprises if so.

A slow rumbling chuckle started in his chest. I looked over at him, eyebrow raised in question. "I was picturing you doing business with Lawrence Caster. It presented an amusing image. Something on you smells like those awful cigars he favors." I just stared back at him, heat rising in my cheeks. "Tell me that's not why you were over there, Grace."

My maintained silence drew heat from the man walking beside me.

"*Grace.* Tell me you weren't trading with that slimy usurer. I'm certain you know better than to deal with people like that."

I simply stared him in the eye. Magnus's jaw clenched, and the vein in his forehead slowly started to pulse. "Fine. I won't tell you then," I responded finally, the words tart on my tongue.

He growled in response, but I just kept walking. I'd be damned if he'd make me feel bad for taking care of business for my family.

CHAPTER 4
MAGNUS

"Does the archmage know?" I reigned in my anger as best I could, but there was still gravel in my voice and my skin itched to turn to stone. Grace wasn't one to flinch, but her eyes snapped to mine at the sharpness of my tone, and she stopped her tense march down the street.

"No, he doesn't. There's no need for him to. This is *my* problem to manage, not his. He's my boss, not my keeper."

Her words were sharp, stinging as they landed on my skin. I had no real business asking, but I couldn't bear the thought of her working with such slime.

"I'm sure he'd like to know that you're visiting a well-known criminal in the Barrens."

She spun, prodding me in the chest with her finger so hard the knuckle blanched white. "Don't you *dare*. My personal life is none of his business. Or yours."

"I wasn't aware you had one of those, to be honest," I teased, cracking a wide smile so I didn't get maimed.

I was smart enough to realize I'd overstepped, though my curiosity wasn't dampened in the least. I wanted to know everything about her, including how she spent her free time. It was an annoying—though not unwelcome—twist in our relationship.

"It's honestly a nice surprise knowing you do," I continued. "I was convinced you only left the grounds to do work-related errands."

Grace scoffed. "Fat lot you know. In any case, what I do on my time is my business. I'm well paid for my work, so don't be trying to spin this around on the archmage. He takes care of me and mine quite well. Better than anyone could ask, in fact. Which is why he's not involved." Grace's eyes traveled up my body and down again, as though she were assessing me for judgment. I straightened my shoulders in response, half tempted to shift into my gargoyle form so she could administer a proper inspection. "My money troubles are none of *your* business either." She turned and started her jog-walking pace once more.

I inhaled through my nose, getting a hint of her freshly-baked-bread-and-honey scent as she gained a small head start, as well as a muddled mix of other people on her clothing.

"They're not even *my* money troubles," she fumed, waving her hands as she talked. "Technically, the debt belongs to my father. He's doing the best he can, all things considered. He can't do most proper work anymore because of his joints, and Mama's already spread too thin with all her little jobs plus caring for him. Cooking, cleaning ... it's all too much. They should be able to enjoy their retirement." She took a deep breath, trying to calm herself as she'd started to rant. "It's just been a slow couple of months. It'll pick up, and we'll be back on track again. We'll figure it out. We always do."

I wasn't sure if she was trying to convince herself or me, but I didn't think either of us was buying it. "Grace, there are other ways—"

She whirled on me, fire and ice in her eyes, the combination potent enough to make me hold my breath. My blood was up, arousal sang in my veins as she charged at me again. "I'm asking you right now to drop it. I'm neither looking for nor accepting handouts. Rylan has taken care of enough. This is *our* issue. We'll handle it."

I had half a mind to go back over there after I saw her safely back home and take care of it myself. I didn't want the stain of Caster's grasp anywhere near her. I knew better, though. The word *independent* didn't quite cover things where Grace was concerned. Forgiveness would be the least of my worries if I overstepped that much—I'd have to wonder about poison in her delicious food for the rest of my days, and that was not a sacrifice I was prepared to make.

Silence dogged our measured steps as the noise of the city fell away and the darkness embraced the streets. Businesses were shuttered, families were inside their homes, resting, and we were finally closing in on the collegium.

"Are you going to follow me the whole way?"

"Yes." I scowled, offended by the question. As if I'd knowingly let her stroll through the city alone after dark. It was bad enough she gallivanted around so boldly during the day, though I knew she was more prepared than most to fend off trouble.

Which reminded me ... I'd have to see if she'd stand for some weapons training. If she wouldn't let me instruct her, perhaps the archmage could handle it. Even one of my daughters might be willing to take her on in their downtime between demon horde exterminations and their other work. If nothing else, Will would certainly be more than happy to supply a new blade.

"Grace," I said with caution, barely a step behind her as she continued to barrel toward the stone building where the collegium was housed.

"What?" she snapped.

"Are you alright?" I asked, both relieved and worried when her pace slowed and she glanced over her shoulder at me.

"I'm fine," she said in a rush, snapping her head back around. "Of course I'm fine. Why would you even ask?"

"No reason." *Every reason.*

She hadn't been the same since Calla's kidnapping, which she seemed to never think of as her own kidnapping, as well. The thought of her being roughed up the way she had been made my blood heat. Anyone who'd touched her in such a way deserved to have their fingers removed as slowly and painfully as possible, just as a start.

Grace hadn't allowed Rylan to use any magic to heal her face, so the deep scrapes she'd gotten had turned into shiny white scars from her temple to her jaw. They were a testament to both her strength and her guilt.

I found they only added to her understated beauty. I also knew I risked life and limb ever mentioning anything like that out loud.

"Do you have knowledge of all the stone kin in the city?" she asked suddenly, surprising me.

"Not all, but many. Why?"

"Just curious."

I knew far better than that. "Who are you inquiring about specifically?" I asked, relieved that we were within sight of the collegium. Once we were inside the iron gates, I might be able to relax a bit.

"Nobody," she sighed, reaching for the latch.

"It doesn't sound like nobody," I countered, but she didn't continue. I lowered my voice, using the softest tone I could manage. "Grace."

Her eyes were pinched as I took the gate in hand, allowing her to enter in front of me. "It's nothing." The words were barely above a whisper, which terrified me.

This woman was bold, loud, and took absolutely no shit from anyone—myself included. I was pretty sure even Rylan bowed to her will. Any woman who had both a demon magus and a gargoyle under her thumb deserved the utmost respect. I loved how she'd spar with me, give me hell, and never back down when she knew she was right.

Quiet meant she doubted herself. Or that she was afraid. Neither of which were acceptable.

"Tell me what's on your mind, Grace. I can't take care of it if I'm in the dark."

She crossed the stones of the courtyard slowly, measuring her words. "I don't need you taking care of things for me, Magnus."

"Of course you don't." I found myself wishing that she did. Because I absolutely wanted to.

She narrowed her eyes at me skeptically. "There are a few working for Caster, is all. I wondered if they were accounted for or just ... wild? They seem young, for the most part, probably part human. Are there enough of you that three or four younglings can work wherever they choose?"

There truly wasn't, especially with the recent uptick in demon horde outbreaks, but I had an idea who she might have seen. Plenty of the younger men in particular thought they'd never burn out and pulled double duty to try to get as much money as they could stashed away. They believed that stone sleep would fix just about anything, and while they weren't wrong, every year they spent doing that would come at a price.

"I'll check into it," I promised, smelling traces of at least three other stone kin on her hair and clothing now that she'd stopped moving and was no longer upwind from me. Her parents were there as well, and a mixture of people she'd probably no more than crossed paths with on the street. I also clearly smelled Caster and his terrible cigars. The scent clung with an oily aftertaste and made me clench my fists.

She fidgeted with the edges of her cloak, making me increasingly nervous about whatever it was she was choosing to keep to herself. "Gaius works for him too. I'm not sure if you know that already, or if you care. But he's there often. And he ..."

"He what?" My voice sharpened again, her tension a direct pull on mine.

I could see the moment she changed her mind and decided to keep something she was about to tell me to herself. Frustration rippled down my spine, tugging at the parts of me that weren't human at all. "Nothing. He's not like you. I'm glad he's not coming around here anymore. I don't trust him."

Her words dropped heavily between us as she turned to go inside the building. I was too stunned by the information to move. There was no reason for her to lie, but what she said didn't make sense. Gaius was a general, just like I was. We had a long, storied history, though I wouldn't call us friends. He had no reason to work for or otherwise engage with a mid-level criminal who catered to the humans of the city like Caster.

So why would he? And how had I not known about it?

CHAPTER 5
GRACE

I LEFT MAGNUS STARING after me and went inside the building. The infuriating man stood in the courtyard, frozen and slack-jawed long after the doors closed behind me. I probably should have felt bad about it. Instead, I reveled in having gotten the upper hand in our interaction, not to mention the last word.

After a quick check that the kitchen had been cleaned and closed down properly, I made my way upstairs. Unlike most of the staff, my rooms were part of a small annex just above the kitchen and dining room. At the top of the stairs was an open storage space where I kept extra dry goods and dishes. I loved the camouflage it provided; basically, nobody knew there was anything else up there. Down a short hall, behind the only door, was my apartment.

It was smaller than the units on the second and third floors, but it was all I needed. I only required somewhere to sleep and recharge myself, and the simple suite covered all my comfort necessities. I had a nook for my bed, a full bathroom with a glorious tub, and a small sitting area. It was perfect.

When the four sisters had first been brought to us, I'd debated moving into one of the newer apartments to be closer to them, but in the end, they'd told me if I was happy where I was that they'd be fine as long as they were together. I was glad for the enduring quiet, if I was being honest. I liked my private little hidden spot close enough to sneak down for a snack if I needed it but out of the way of student traffic. The heavy stone walls dampened all the noise as well. It was my own cozy little nook, and I loved it.

My shoes were the first thing to come off, then my cloak and gown. I all but dove into the tub once the water was running, not even waiting for it to fill first. The smell of cigars and desperation had to go. It clung to my hair and skin, making me feel as dirty as the money Lawrence traded around.

Less than a year and we'd be free. I only had to scrape together enough to make full payments until the end. I already had an idea for what I could do to supplement my income, though it meant less sleep and more secrets.

I leaned back in the hot water, rolling the events of the day around in my head as my muscles relaxed. Nothing had gone quite as I'd expected, especially the part where I ran into Magnus down in the Barrens.

He and I had a volatile chemistry that presented as friendly sarcasm most of the time. I knew he was a good man with a heart of solid gold. The friendship he and the archmage had went further back than I could even dream of conceptualizing, which told me all I needed to know. Rylan himself was a true gem, and any friend of his was alright in my book.

Behind my closed eyelids I pictured Magnus. While outwardly he looked to be vaguely middle-aged, I knew he was actually centuries old. In his human form, he was a towering, broadly built man with tanned skin and brown eyes. His dark hair had a gentle curl to it and often curtained his eyes since he didn't cut it nearly as often as he should. He was objectively beautiful, and the multitude of scars and his crooked smile only enhanced his attractiveness.

In his stone form, he was even larger and somehow more handsome, both of which should have been impossible. I'd seen his wide bat-like wings with bone spear points at the end, fangs, and lions-paw feet plenty of times. While an imposing figure, he never frightened me. Quite the opposite, in fact. I worried that perhaps he should at least make me cautious when he was in his broad stone form with weapons built into parts of his body ... but he was not like Gaius. I'd seen the way Magnus went out of his way to treat people with kindness and acceptance. Heard him speak lovingly of his children and the mate he'd lost well before I'd met him. Watched him pull Calla into his family, calling her his niece when their blood might not be the same at all.

The heart that beat in Magnus's chest was undoubtedly soft ... perhaps the only soft thing about him.

I shook myself out of the daydreamy state as the water started to cool and realized my hand had slid low on my stomach. I frowned at how easily I'd started to romanticize the bottomless pit of a man it was often my job to feed. The frustration he caused me by dropping in and out was not negligible. He required a separate food budget all to himself, and more than once, he and Rylan had roughhoused themselves through a number of student dining tables.

My mouth twitched into a smile as I mentally scolded them for being overgrown children. In truth, it was nice to see that side of such a man. Growing that old could leave a person entirely too serious.

I combed the snarls out of my hair after pulling on a nightgown, my memories happily replaying moments that featured Magnus. Exhaustion tugged at my limbs by the time I was finished brushing my teeth, my mind too tired to construct the story I might need around my best option for supplementing the payments for Lawrence.

As I lay in bed, cozy under what was an embarrassing number of blankets, I reminded myself not to worry, that there was a way. I'd figure it out. I always did.

A FEW DAYS later, the archmage and his new wife departed the collegium for an extended vacation. They hadn't taken a honeymoon right after their wedding since classes had still been in session. Now that it was summer and there were no students to worry about, and he'd finally given in to our collective insistence that it was okay for him to leave. I think it helped that both Rylan's own brother, Vassago, and Magnus would both be around to keep an eye on things.

Vassago was much like the archmage, so planning for meals wouldn't be difficult. He was kind enough, though he mostly kept to himself when he wasn't practicing his mystical arts in one of the classrooms.

Magnus had an apartment in the faculty hall as well, but he only used it some of the time. He alternated between his apartment, sleeping up in the tower observatory, and some other location around the city I wasn't privy to. His business kept him on the move, and it was none of mine.

With less demand on me in the evening, I could finally proceed with my plans to locate the men who'd kept me in the warehouse that day. Rylan would have either forbid it or tried to help, so with him gone, I felt safer putting my twofold plan into action without guilt or interference.

"After supper I need you to clean and close," I instructed Sara. "Alright?"

She nodded, smiling at the implied increase responsibility. "Yes ma'am."

"You and your sisters can take some snacks to your room, of course. Just be smart."

"I understand, Ms. Grace."

"Good girl. Make sure Bridget knows she can stop doing that wash once it's time for dinner, okay? She doesn't have to go back to finish. There's always going to be more for her to do. Her poor little fingers are going to wrinkle up and fall off if she doesn't give them a chance to dry out."

Sara giggled. "I will."

As she scuttled off to collect her sisters for dinner, our resident posh, fair demon ambled into the dining room.

"Grace," Vassago said with a gentle smile, inclining his head slightly as he approached.

"Mr. Feland. What can I do for you?"

"Please, call me by my name. There's no need for formality between us."

"As you wish. How can I help you, Vassago?"

He smiled. "Could I trouble you for some wine and a few things to eat in my room?"

"Of course, that's quickly becoming my specialty," I teased. "Give me just a moment, and I'll put something together for you. Unless you'd like to come into the kitchen?"

He seemed nervous by this suggestion, which amused me to no end. The men were all terrified to encroach on what they considered my domain, though I'd never even once brandished a knife at them in threat. Not that I could recall, anyway.

"Would you mind?"

"Not at all. You can tell me what you like, and I'll be sure to keep it around."

"That would be lovely, thank you."

Like his brother, he was well over six feet tall. There was something about the men who gravitated to this building being oversized. Likely it was something to do with their lack of human genetics, but that was just a guess.

I pulled out another big basket and started to pack it with dishes. He selected a bottle of wine from the rack, and then I moved on to food. "This platter was prepared for Calla," I said, poking around in the ice box. "With them gone, you're welcome to it. Cheeses and meats, mostly. I usually just send up a whole tin of crackers or a loaf of bread. There's some fruit and even some vegetables if you like. Cookies? Cakes? Your preference."

I looked at the man whose light-gold eyes had widened, clearly overwhelmed. "Ah … whatever you'd send for them is fine, I don't want to be any extra trouble."

I smiled and nodded reassuringly, packed the basket to the brim, and handed it off to him. He had a place to put it in his suite, so I knew it wouldn't go bad before he ate it all. "There you are."

"Thank you, Grace."

"You're welcome to come find me or pilfer the pantry at your leisure. Just make a note if you take the last of something so I know to add it to the market list."

"Certainly."

I saw him hesitate. "Is there something else?"

He actually blushed, which was truly something to see. "I've invited a visitor to come tour the campus. A chemist. I don't know how often she'll be here. Just thought it worth mentioning, I don't want to put you to extra trouble unnecessarily."

"How lovely! I'm excited to meet her. We can always use new brilliance around here. I'll be sure to have an extra serving or two built into my plans, though I never seem to make too much, no matter how much I pad the menu."

He bowed out with a thanks, leaving me in the quiet room by myself. I prepared the girls' dinner, snacking as I went. I was too nervous to eat a whole meal myself, mainly because of where I planned to go. Taking the opportunity presented, I stole up to my room and gathered my things, heart thumping nervously behind my ribs.

I was really doing this.

When I got back downstairs, the girls were busily eating their meals at one of the long bench tables. I reminded them again to clean and close, then slipped out into the hall. Before I could change my mind, I continued on until I was out the doors, then the courtyard gate, headed into the center of town for the second time in a week.

CHAPTER 6
MAGNUS

Following grace into the city under the cover of darkness had quickly become quite the bad habit. It had been pure luck that I'd seen her leaving the campus grounds that first night, but now it was part of my evening routine to see if she wandered back into the city after supper.

While patrolling the city at night was technically my responsibility, perching myself on a bakery's roof to watch her work the evening away at a beer garden certainly was not. I'd been a soldier for centuries, but I'd be damned if I was going to prioritize some questionable merchant practices over finding out what this infuriating woman was trying to do by going to such a place. Alone. At night. In secret. To *work*. Besides, I was a general. I was the one who doled out the patrol assignments, and she was now my number one priority.

I flew among the shadows as long as I could, the flare of her skirts a beacon below me. When space became too limited for me to fly between the cramped buildings near the center of town, I leapt from roof to roof, careful not to disturb the occupants inside. More than once, I'd accidentally knocked over an entire row of heavy clay flower pots or a laundry line and the whole neighborhood had come out to investigate. I was quick, stealthy, but some situations were difficult to escape or explain.

Grace's hooded form ducked into the beer garden as I settled into the shadows, spreading my weight evenly across the clay tiles of the roof. She made a quick change in a nook to one side of the food booth, leaving her cloak behind as she donned an apron and began waiting tables. She carted trays of heavy steins of beer, sausages on sticks, and platters of pastries, collecting coins as tips and watching the crowds as though she were looking for someone in particular.

There was one waitress I was certain she was trying to get eyes on, though the chances of that were slim to none. The woman who had colluded with the kidnappers was undoubtedly long gone, I was certain of it. However, there were at least a few patrons I was sure she also hoped to recognize.

I had half a mind to scold her soundly for such reckless behavior, but I also understood it. The guilt over what happened the day they were kidnapped was probably eating her alive. This was a way to soothe it. Knowing she had business with Caster was a reasonable explanation for why she'd taken on a second job as well.

Rylan would be mortified. Furious. He'd almost certainly visit the Barrens himself to settle the debt. She'd never forgive him if he did.

I didn't know what it meant for me that I had the exact same intention. I merely had to figure out a way to make it so she didn't despise me afterward.

I monitored her behavior from my perch, noting anyone who held her interest for longer than a few moments, and kept an eye on those who seemed likely to start trouble. After the heavy dinner crowd thinned, Grace took a much-needed break.

She sat at one of the vacant tables closest to the entrance, just as she had the previous several nights. She never ordered any ale, though she'd gotten a cup of mead the night before. She watched both patrons and waitstaff alike from her table as she picked a pastry apart flake by flake, leaving half of it as crumbs in the dirt for the birds to find.

I crept closer to the edge of the roof and got comfortable, settling in for the long haul as she went back to work. A trio of men ambled in and took a seat near the middle of the garden, immediately making my neck prickle. They were loud, went through three rounds of drinks in a regrettably short amount of time, and nobody wanted to serve them past a single round for several obvious reasons: They were terrible tippers and some of the most demanding customers present. They lingered for over an hour, getting progressively messy. One grabbed at a waitress's ass and got thumped over the head with her tray as a reward. Another decided to offer his coin by flicking it high in the air to see if they could catch it.

When the rest of the servers were fed up with them, Grace, as one of the newest members of the transient staff, was made to take over. Every nerve I had flared to life as I watched her stiffen when she approached their table. It was enough discomfort to make my skin itch.

I hated to take my eyes off of her for even a moment, but she was blocked from my view as I slipped from the roof, scaling quickly down the side of the bakery. By the time I got to the entrance of the beer garden, she was already gone. I glanced around and found the flare of her cloak as she swept beyond the edge of the garden and into the shadows.

Deciding that the men were my priority and I'd catch up to her, I took a deep breath and joined them. "Hello, boys," I said, smiling widely as I dropped my body onto the bench at their table.

"Do we know you?" one asked, swaying slightly in his seat.

"No, we don't know each other. Yet."

Their brash energy settled as they looked back and forth between themselves. Fear rolled off them, an acrid smell doused in the hoppy ale and garlic of the sausages. I was blessed with a stomach of steel, but it made me wish my sense of smell wasn't quite so keen.

I pulled out a coin and set it on the table, garnering their dedicated interest. "I'm looking for information," I said, forcing a placid smile despite itching to simply start a fight. I clenched one fist in my lap, the other hand flat on the table top.

"Information?" the one I was beginning to recognize as the leader, since he was the one to speak up, asked.

"Yes. About a warehouse."

"Lots of those in this city," he grumbled, slurping down his drink. When it was empty, he held the glass above his head to signal he needed a waitress to come refill it.

"The one I'm looking for had a woman in it a few months back."

The quietest one started to laugh. He barked several beats' worth of a rough chuckle, then stopped. When he started up again, the others joined in.

"Lots of those around too," the leader said.

Patience at an end, my worry for Grace hit a peak, as she was likely halfway home already. I reached out and snatched his shirt at the collar. "It's important," I said, voice dangerously low.

His two sidekicks shifted nervously as he grabbed at my arm. "Alright, alright. No need to get worked up."

I relaxed my grip, and he snatched the coin from the table, beads of sweat dotting his forehead. His dark eyes grew shifty. A waitress had yet to stop by with more ale, and I was certain they wouldn't until I'd left. "We just do as we're told," he said, holding his hands out in front of him.

"That's a lie," I countered.

"Hey, man." His eyes went wide as they took me in. "Listen, we don't mean no harm—"

"That's also a lie, and I'm growing *very* impatient." I inhaled deeply, looking between them. They were all still and silent, nervousness having overtaken their drunken bravery. "A woman was taken from here while eating a meal with her mistress. To a warehouse. She was left overnight. Treated most unkindly before being sent on her way. I need to know who all was involved. And from the sound of it, how often that kind of thing happens."

"Sure, sure. I mean, it's possible that's something we might have been paid to do, but I see a lot of women, you know? I'm not sure I'd recognize—"

My fist snapped out, and his nose broke with a satisfying crunch under my knuckles. Blood blossomed around his hand as he gripped his face. I wasn't eased by the action as I'd hoped. If anything, it had only served to stoke my need for violence. Now that I'd drawn first blood, I wanted it all.

"Hey! C'mon, man!" The other two got to their feet, and in a few swift motions, I had them all by the collar, dragging them from the beer garden into the alley beyond.

Inflicting as much pain as possible was on my mind, but getting the information was more important. For now. They spilled the names and addresses I asked for without much further provocation, much to my disappointment. All it took was a cuff on the ear to bring them to their knees, begging, like the spineless garbage they were. The only consolation was that they'd be on my list to visit in the very near future. Their survival was only guaranteed for the short term, though they had no idea about that.

With assurances that they'd keep our conversation to themselves, they scuttled off into the night, metaphorical tails between their legs. I took to the roofs to locate Grace, blood singing with a fierce combination of rage and the desire to protect her. Hopping from building to building, I released my wings, allowing the cool night air to buffet against me, hoping it would cool me off before I found her.

If it didn't ... we were both in for some trouble.

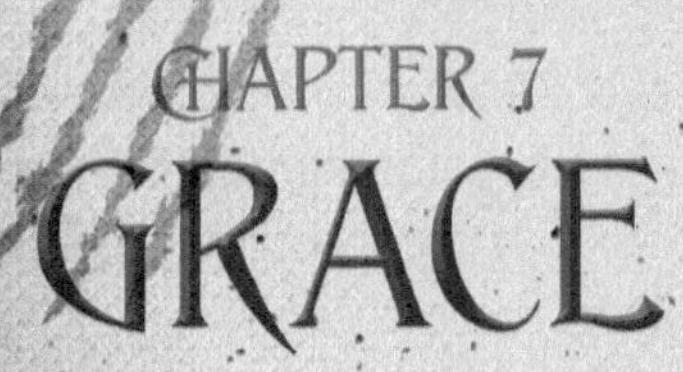

CHAPTER 7
GRACE

IT TOOK EVERY ounce of willpower I had to calmly collect my pay for the night, turn in my apron, and leave the beer garden. My hands trembled, my breath rattled in my chest as I made my feet carry me away from the men I recognized. They'd drugged me and left me for dead in a warehouse across town. I was unreasonably proud I'd managed to serve them and leave without either screaming at them or breaking down.

Everyone had a story to tell about them once I'd asked. Before I'd been rotated in to serve them, some of the other waitresses had given me additional information about where they thought the men worked most of the time and had summarized their various offenses from previous visits.

It was enough. It had to be.

As I reached the first corner, relief teased at the edges of my awareness. I sucked in the first full breath I'd been able to manage since seeing the men laughing without a care over their ale. Then I promptly ran headlong into a very large, firm body.

"Sorry," I muttered, but my blood turned to ice as I looked up and met a stern gaze. He was the last person, aside from the three in the beer garden, that I wanted to see.

"No harm done." He ran his tongue along his teeth as he stared down at me, my spine straightening in response.

"Gaius." I stepped to the side, trying to dart around him. "Apologies again. I'll just be on my way."

His heavy palm dropped onto my shoulder. "What's the hurry, love?"

"I'm late getting back. If you don't mind ..." It wasn't a total lie—I always had plenty to do back at the collegium. I was proud that my voice was firm. I even managed to lift an eyebrow in defiance. "The archmage is expecting me." He most certainly was not, especially considering he wasn't even in the city, but Gaius didn't know that. Hopefully.

His piercing blue gaze narrowed, unrelenting as he searched my soul for the truth of my words. "We wouldn't want to keep him waiting, now would we? Don't be a stranger, Grace. See you in a couple of weeks at the very least." His hand slipped from my shoulder, making a detour through my hair as I dipped my head politely.

I went all the way across the street to get distance from him before continuing on. As my feet traveled along the cobblestones, the hair on my neck bristled. My skin prickled, and I felt edgy. I had to stuff my hands in my pockets and force myself to face forward. I knew if I looked over my shoulder, I'd find him still watching me.

My hood slipped from my hair as I glanced up. I sucked in a breath when I found a hulking dark shadow with broad wings racing along the rooftops beside me. The quick glimpse told me all I needed to know for panic to truly set in. Gaius hadn't let me go. He was following me.

I knew Revalia like the back of my hand, but in the dark, with lamps few and far between, I didn't care to cut through the city using my usual back alley or skinny side road shortcuts.

"C'mon, Grace, pick up your feet," I chided myself, gathering great handfuls of skirt as I pushed my legs to move just a little faster.

I turned right after passing a few more streets, deciding that my best route was through the woods that connected the collegium to the back of a residential part of town to save some time. And maybe I could lose my tail if I got lucky.

My chest burned with every breath as I went into a full run when the trees came into view. Plunging into the cover they offered, I wound through the massive old oaks, the moonlight the only illumination along my twisted path. Gnarled branches tore at my skirts, my face, my arms, but I didn't slow down. The shadow was now directly above me, outlined by the bright white of the full moon like a dark angel.

I knew better.

He was no angel, and he was not to be trusted.

Cursing myself for being such a fool—*again*—I gulped down painful gasps of air as my feet ate up the distance between the edge of the city and the back of d'Arcan. I had no plan for what to do when I got there aside from hurl myself inside the doors, but that sounded like salvation in the present moment.

I could see the iron fencing of the horse paddock and nearly cried in relief. The beat of the heavy wings had grown closer, and I felt the dark shadow of him pressing along my back. Arms pumping, I raced across the dirt, prepared to hurdle the fence if need be.

All at once, the earth rose up to meet me as a heavy body crashed into me from behind. We tumbled through the leaves and under-brush, the large form plastered to my back, stone arms banded around my center. He took the brunt of the fall, I realized, as leaves and rocks skittered past my vision but left me unscathed. I hadn't even lost my breath in the fall.

"Let me go!" I cursed, flailing my limbs uselessly against his grip.

"If you promise to stop running from me, I will," the familiar voice grumbled, hot against my neck.

I froze, turning my head as far as it would go. To one side of us were trees, on the other, a collection of rounded boulders well over a man's height.

"Magnus?"

"I'd also appreciate it very much if you'd stop wiggling." He exhaled tightly, and I realized that it was no sword hilt I felt along my backside.

Pulling myself out of his grasp, I sat up and smacked him solidly on the shoulder. It was a useless effort, especially as he was still in full gargoyle form, but it made me feel better. "What in the name of all the saints are you doing *chasing* me like that? You nearly gave me a heart attack."

"I could ask you the same," he grunted out while checking me over for damage. His broad fingertips swept across my skin, making it dance with a ripple of gooseflesh. A number of nicks and cuts made themselves known as he did his inspection, his frown deepening with each one he found.

"What's got you so scared you're running through the woods at night? *Alone?*"

"You!" I spat back, getting to my feet and brushing the leaves from my dress. "You were following me! *Chasing* me. I thought—" I hesitated, unsure if I wanted to share my fear about his friend quite yet. I had no idea how he'd react to such an accusation.

Magnus climbed to his full height, wings extended, before leaning forward and sniffing at my neck. His motions pressed my back against one of the rounded boulders.

"What are you—"

His pupils, already larger than I'd ever seen them, dilated so wide only a sliver of the dark chocolate color around the edge remained. "Why do you smell of Gaius? Why has he touched you? Touched what's *mine*? *Again*?"

My brain stuttered over his words; my pulse kicked into a painful throb in my throat. Things between us had always been … unique, but that declaration added a whole new dimension. "I—"

Magnus reached up to cup my cheek with his broad palm, his long fingers wrapping around to the back of my neck. I watched in what felt like slow motion as his face came increasingly closer. "Mine." With a growl, Magnus sealed his lips to mine.

Everything else ceased to exist as I was overtaken by the taste of ozone and fresh spearmint, his razor-sharp fangs delicately teasing along my bottom lip as he sipped at my mouth like a dying man who'd been gifted his favorite drink. His arousal pressed into my stomach, a low throb echoing in the hollow between my legs in response. Thoughts were impossible to gather as my back curved into the boulder. I was trapped between a massive rock and a giant of a man who was somehow the harder of the two objects.

"Yours?" I asked, when he finally released me, intoxicated by the rush of endorphins floating around in my blood. I hadn't been kissed in years, and I'd *never* been kissed like this. The passion he poured into me … I couldn't possibly be held responsible for my reaction to such a potent thing. Everything in me reached right for him.

"I'm sure you're gearing up for a speech about how you belong to no one," he started, placing the pads of his fingers against my lips as I opened them to protest. I wasn't doing any such thing, despite how I should have been. His eyes were fixed on that part of my face, as though he was prepared to devour me all over again. "But you just made me chase you through the forest. I cannot *breathe* over my desire for you, Grace. So I'm telling you now, you're mine. Am I yours? Do you want this?"

The moan that came out of my throat would have horrified me at any other moment. As it was, I saw it ignite something in his eyes, and I further dissolved into a puddle of need. What would it be like to have claim over such a man? A soldier who could dispatch any enemy with barely a thought. A thoughtful friend who cared for those he loved with all he had. A literal mountain who could choose human skin or statue form, both equally and uniquely beautiful.

I shivered, the notion of it all overwhelming, especially with him so close. "Yes," I whispered, curiosity and desire overtaking caution.

Magnus rumbled deep in his throat as he placed one of his broad hands on each of my ass cheeks. He pulled me upward, forcing me to wrap my legs around his middle as he pressed my back into the boulder. His mouth meshed with mine and his impressive, hard cock aligned with my center.

A squeak of surprise left my throat as I melted into his embrace. One of his hands traveled along my thigh, gripping firmly as it climbed toward my core. The other slid along my cheek until his fingertips were tangled in my curls and protecting the back of my head from the stone behind me.

As our mouths twined and he pressed himself further into the vee of my legs, I found myself wholly shocked by the notion that I was at peace. Everything in my head was quiet. My heart was a stuttering mess in my chest, but this felt more natural than it had any right to.

It was a heady feeling to be so wanted by someone, so free in the moment. I wasn't sure I'd ever felt this way before, not even when I was young and wild. Giving up any semblance of control I kept over myself was a *relief*. The strange new twist our relationship had taken was not, in fact, a surprise but rather seemed like a foregone conclusion that had finally come to pass.

I realized that all those times we'd bickered and swiped at one another might actually have amounted to extended foreplay. This moment was the culmination of all that and then some.

It had never occurred to me to desire such a thing, but I'd suddenly never wanted anything more.

CHAPTER 8
MAGNUS

GRACE WAS NOT a petite woman, but having her trapped below me in my stone form left her far less domineering than usual. I knew it might be one of the few times I could truly claim to have the upper hand with her. If I was honest with myself, I liked it that way.

I loved that she had no compunction about putting me in my place. I would revel in the few moments I was given the honor of putting her in hers. The primal part of me that recognized someone running away as nothing more than prey to be hunted had been fully stimulated as she led me on the chase through the woods. Knowing it was her I was flying after had turned my need to draw blood into something else entirely. Certainly not less intense ... just different.

"Grace." I breathed her name, and the heat of my breath against her neck caused her to shiver. Her pulse fluttered in her throat, the scent of her blood, her arousal ... everything that was *her* filled my senses. Regrettably, there was still a trace of Gaius lingering as well. My deep inhale spurred a fresh surge of desire and rage to rush through my blood. She moaned as I traced my tongue along the curve of her throat. "I cannot shift back yet."

She was warm against me, even through the layers of our clothing. "What does that mean?" Her voice was breathy as she blinked up at me, hazel eyes glossy with lust. That normally sharp-tongued mouth was open, drawing my attention to rosy, swollen lips from our kisses. Grace perched her hands on my shoulders, the soft touch of her fingers added a separate layer of fiery electricity running through my skin.

I hadn't wanted anything the way I wanted her. Not for *years*.

"This is the version of me you'll be getting. In all ways." I choked on my words as she ground herself against me.

"I like this version of you just fine." She raised an eyebrow, chuckling playfully at me. "Even when you eat a full week's worth of groceries in one sitting, I might actually like this version better. It's hard to be angry with your pretty human face sometimes."

"Pretty?"

"Mmm."

Her hands moved, tracing along the edges of my wings, the sharp bone points hovering near her sides as the appendages sheltered her and balanced me.

She wiggled, trying to find a more comfortable spot against the boulder.

"Grace," I hissed, cock throbbing.

"Magnus?" My name became an invitation as it rolled off her lips.

"I cannot offer gentleness," I warned. "Or control."

"I never asked."

I snarled, tearing away her undergarments with my claws before unlashing the fastenings of my trousers. Bared to the air, her scent surrounded me. I ran my thumb along her wet slit, reveling in the way her back arched up and her chest rattled with a moan. "Do you like to be chased, little rabbit?" I circled her clit with the digit, which caused her hips to twitch. "Do you like to be scared?"

"Not scared," she gasped.

"But chased," I confirmed. "That works out rather well for the both of us." Any answer she might have been preparing to give was cut off into by a groan as I sank my thumb into her heat. Her body was warm, slick, and pliable, cupping around me greedily. "Fuck, Grace."

"You should," she panted.

"Should what?"

"Fuck Grace."

She'd be the end of me, I was sure of it.

I rubbed my thumb along the soft spot at the front of her, eliciting another twitch of her hips before removing my hand and stroking her wetness along the head of my cock. Head bowed over hers, I sought confirmation in her eyes. What I found there was an echo of my own desire, of my very soul.

One of her hands gripped the curled end of my wing spear, her heels dug into my ass as she pulled me closer to her body. "Please," she sighed, tongue darting out to moisten her lips.

I exhaled and surged forward, melding my mouth to hers as I pressed against her entrance.

"Wait," she gasped, and despite the drive to plunder her body, to make it mine immediately, I stilled.

"What's wrong?"

"Even just as a man you're quite a bit larger than most. As this version of yourself ... I'm not sure ..."

"Speak clearly, Grace." I was hazy with lust, the temptation close enough to touch. As such, the tenuous grasp I had on my control slipped further away.

"I don't think you're going to fit," she panted, eyes wide as she felt me there. Her body tensed, the muscles preventing easy entrance.

"Not to worry, Little Rabbit." I felt the dark descent into my more beastly form take over, gravel in my voice as her words flattered my ego. "You can take it. I'd never hurt you."

She nodded, but the tension was still there. I stroked down her face with my fingers, then moved lower along her body, teasing at the sides of her breasts, the stiff peak of her nipple, and the hollow of her waist. I kissed her deeply, tangling my tongue with hers, inhaling her flavor and relishing the fact that my attention garnered a fresh wave of wetness between her legs.

On a sigh, Grace angled her body so she could accept my intrusion more readily, and we swallowed one another's breath as I slid inside. Thought became nothing more than white static as my cock pulsed, the sheath of her body tight against the length of me.

"You were made for me, Grace," I muttered, sipping at her lips as my hips began to move. I put both hands under her head, protecting her from the stone at her back as I sank into her over and over again. Her slickness spread along my length as her body cradled mine in a tight embrace.

Her hands struggled to settle on a place to grab onto as I gave over to the mindless thrusting my body demanded. They flitted from my face, to my wing tips, to my shoulders, and back again. I didn't care where she touched, it all sent a thrill through me. Eventually, she gripped my forearms, finding the leverage she'd been seeking as her body began to throb around me.

"Magnus." Her head rolled to the side, her eyes squeezed closed. Her body tightened around me, and I canted my hips so my pelvis would apply more pressure where I was sure she craved it most.

She cried out, and my hips snapped faster against her as I felt the rush of wetness from her climax ease the friction of my thrusts. The sound of our heavy breaths and the slap of flesh meeting flesh echoed into the cool night, quieting even the animals as we disappeared into the moment together.

"Again," I demanded, the sound a snarl in my throat. My cock jumped as she sank her fingernails into my arms.

"I can't," she whined.

"You can. You will."

Shifting my hands, I dropped one between us, gathering her moisture before rubbing against her clit in slow, firm circles. I felt her pulse throb in the network of veins there, smelled the way her scent changed as the tension began to build again. My own need sang as a tight heat originated in the base of my spine, spiraling outward.

Her legs spasmed and clenched at my sides as an orgasm took her again. While she pulsed around me, I dropped my head down, focus narrowed to her blissed-out face as I fell into my own release. I roared, pressing myself into her as far as I could go as heat shot through my veins and left me depleted.

Sagging against her, I marveled over what had become of us. I dipped to kiss her throat again and found she was damp with sweat despite the chill in the air. I licked along her collarbone, reveling in her salted honey flavor. I couldn't wait to taste all of her. "Well done, Little Rabbit. I knew you had it in you," I praised her, kissing gently along her cheeks.

"That makes one of us," she said. The corners of her mouth twitched up as she fought to catch her breath.

I knew right then, covered in sweat and the result of our coupling, that I was in trouble.

Grace was mine. I was hers.

My soul would never be the same.

AFTER WE COLLECTED ourselves, I walked Grace the rest of the way home. I managed to shift back into my human form as we got closer. Somewhere between the boulders and the clearing around the campus property, she'd gone quiet, and turned inward. I hated it.

She stopped outside the main doors of the building, as though we were on some awkward first date and she was about to give me a kiss on the cheek and send me on my way.

"I'd better get inside. The girls ..." She looked guiltily away from me.

"The girls are fine. I checked on them earlier and Vago is down the hall from their apartment. Let's get a nightcap, hmm?" I opened the door, gesturing for her to go inside.

"Oh. Alright." The blush on her cheeks revived the embers of my lust. It was going to be very difficult to get anything done if my hormones decided I was reverting back to my younger years. Much, *much* younger years.

Grace flitted around the kitchen, piling up my favorite little honey cakes on a plate. "Did you want wine?" she asked.

"This is fine," I said, making quick work of a handful of the sweet confections. She ate one as well, avoiding my eyes. "Grace."

"Hmm?"

"Are you alright?"

She blushed again, but nodded. "Yes, I'm fine. It's just been ... a while. I'm not sure how this part goes."

"This part?"

Grace gestured her arms widely, then waved her hand between our bodies. "After. This. What comes next."

I tilted my head to the side, catching some of her loose curls in my fingers as I crowded into her body. She tensed but held her ground, looking up at me. "We are the same as we were before, Grace. Just ... more."

"More."

"Yes." I dipped down, pressing my lips to her forehead.

"Okay," she whispered.

We picked at the cakes, spoke about plans for the day, the week ... anything but discuss the topic looming over us. "We need to talk about what happened tonight," I prompted. "Among other things."

"I know."

She wasn't forthcoming, so I didn't press. "You need to get some rest. So do I. It's late, and you know how I need my beauty sleep."

She snorted and gave me the smile I'd been hoping for. "I do. Breakfast will be coming very early, I have a feeling."

"I'm sorry for robbing you of your rest time," I apologized. "But not for anything else."

"Me neither," she said quietly.

Relief washed over me. Rejection was not something I was familiar with, mostly because I didn't offer myself up for it often. It would have been painful for her to regret our coupling. Guilt would have eaten me from the inside out, and I wouldn't have forgiven myself for not only hurting her but ruining our friendship.

She put away our leftovers and cleaned up, leaving us staring at one another again in the quiet kitchen. "For what it's worth, I don't know how this part goes either," I finally said, wrapping my arms around her. Grace sagged into my embrace in a way that gave me great relief.

I knew all too well she didn't lean on anyone or ask for help unless she absolutely couldn't get by without it. She was one of the strongest, most capable people I'd ever met. For her to trust me enough to relax into my arms was a tremendous honor. I didn't take it lightly.

"Good night, Magnus," she said, pulling away.

"Good night, Grace."

I watched her go through the back of the kitchen, her footsteps above my head as she went into her hidden apartment. Turning out lights as I went, I made my way through the collegium to my own apartment, wondering if the day would come again where I'd share a living space with a woman.

If it did, I wanted it to be her.

CHAPTER 9
GRACE

THE ANNOYINGLY HANDSOME man was watching me with a coy grin over the top of his pitcher of coffee. Beast. The nerve he had to be in such a cheerful mood when I was positively stewing over what had happened the night before.

Not in a bad way. More in a *How did we get here?* kind of way. Maybe even an *Are we going to continue, because I could be really good at making that a bad habit* kind of way.

His abnormally large hands made regular cups look like something a child would use. Or a doll. Meals required multiple plates or platters and drinks were often offered to him directly from the serving container. Coffee was no different, though I hadn't intended for him to drink directly out of my best ceramic carafe.

"Don't you have somewhere you should be? Perhaps in the observatory as a statue, still getting that beauty rest you spoke of?"

He snorted, leaning back arrogantly in his chair. "I'm quite well rested, thank you. And I know better than to let you out of my sight. We have things to talk about, and if I'm not right here"—he mimed me walking away with his fingers—"you'll slip out into the city, and I'll be stuck here with all these questions." His voice dipped to a teasing growl. "Though I could always chase you down."

I pinned him with a stare, desperate to ignore the pulse between my legs. In response to my silence, I got a wide smile and raised eyebrow. And damn my hormones anyway—especially the way they responded to his cockiness. That throbbing only reminded me I was indeed a bit sore from our interlude. Blood rushed to my cheeks, heating my whole face, and that irritated me too. "Fine. Are you wanting to eat my food then?"

His tongue traveled along his lower lip, and I cursed myself for leaving an opening like that. "I can think of several things I have an appetite for," he said, gravel in his voice as his hand tightened around the coffee container.

"I'm afraid we're only offering eggs and toast this morning." I slapped the table irritably and headed off to the kitchen to get us both a plate, his low chuckle chasing me the whole way.

To my immense relief, Vassago had joined him by the time I returned. I deposited the plates in front of them, gladly taking the excuse his arrival gave me to dash back to the kitchen. As I took a few deep breaths, willing myself to stop sweating, my littlest helper, Jana, came scuttling in with the dirty dishes she and her sisters had created with their own meals.

"Mr. Vago would like some coffee. I told him I would get it," she said brightly.

"That's a good helper, Jana, thank you. Did you need anything more to eat?"

"No ma'am. I'm going to help Clem with the horses after this." She focused on not spilling as she poured a steaming cup from the large pot on the stove.

"Well done. I'll see you later on." She nodded and left as quickly as she'd come, and I was stuck alone to decide what I could stomach.

Just as I was plating up the eggs I'd boiled for myself, Magnus's voice boomed across the dining hall, calling my name. "If you don't come back and join us, I'll come in there to retrieve you."

"You wouldn't dare," I whispered to myself, grabbing a fork. "No need to get cranky," I scolded once I got on the other side of the kitchen door, "I was only making myself a plate."

"Mmm," he grumbled, eyebrow raised in gentle accusation. Vassago looked between us, settling on a conspiratorial smile as his gaze returned to his breakfast. "I have an appointment with a handful of merchants today. Would you care to join me, demon?"

The fair man turned to the gargoyle, eyes narrowed. "What kind of meeting?"

"I believe I'll be recruiting a few new members for camp."

My heart dipped, my fork scraping painfully against my plate. "The work camp?"

Magnus inclined his head in answer as he shoveled eggs into his mouth with a slice of toast.

"I could be convinced," Vassago nodded. "I have to be back by the afternoon, though. I have a guest coming."

"Shouldn't take long. I'll need to make a stop back here on my way out of town anyway."

"Dare I ask?" I looked between them.

"You know what kind of people end up in the camp," Magnus shrugged, though he seemed unusually pleased with himself.

"Yes, I do, which is why I'm concerned." The Marchand girls' parents had been the last recruits for the camps I was aware of. I knew exactly what kind of people ended up there. Only the worst kind.

"What kind of guest?" Magnus asked abruptly, as though what Vassago had said finally registered.

"Is it the chemist you mentioned?" I asked, glad to have any sliver of information Magnus didn't. I knew my irritation with him wasn't healthy or even rational, but it's how we operated most of the time. It was the normalcy I needed to balance my emotions this morning.

"Yes, she's coming to tour the campus."

"She?" Magnus teased, his smile broad.

"Yes, *she*." Vassago finished his breakfast with a polite dab of his mouth with his napkin. Looking every inch a regal lord, he leaned back in the seat with his coffee cradled between his hands. "I'm betting she'll be either a good candidate to be a student, or perhaps a good addition to the staff. I believe her to be stone kin, as well."

"This I'd love to see. We'll be back as soon as possible," Magnus promised.

As the men made off to collect their quarry, I cleaned up and prepared for my trip to the market. Just as I was headed out the doors with my list, they were coming back in, three stocky men in tow.

I blanched, my stomach giving a mighty lurch as I recognized them. That in itself was no easy feat as they'd been beaten quite severely already.

"Magnus," I said, tearing my eyes away from the bruised faces. His expression was blank, and it was like I was looking at someone else entirely.

"You don't have to worry about them anymore," he said simply, voice raspy as though he were partially in his stone form despite the human face he wore. "I've brought them here so you could see for yourself. They're no longer a threat to you. They never will be again, I swear it."

"How did you ..." I stopped, ice in my veins as it clicked together.

He'd been following me last night. All night. Not just into the woods. I wanted to be angry about it but couldn't quite muster the emotion over the relief that I no longer had to look over my shoulder or seek these men out.

Vassago stood off to the side, looking thoughtful. Magnus had smears of blood on his face, hands, and clothing. Somehow, the demon had none. His silver vest and white shirt were as pristine as ever. How he'd managed that was a mystery, because I would have put good money on some of the bruises belonging to his fists.

Magnus shoved them all to their knees in the dirt, each of their heads lolling back on their necks as he grasped them by the hair. "Apologize to her."

The first man's mouth pinched tight. The second began to snivel, fat tears rolling down his face. The third spat on the ground at my feet.

"Now, that's not very nice." Vassago cuffed the third one soundly in the temple with the hilt of his sword. He looked more than dazed, pupils wide as he blinked through the pain and probable concussion.

"They're much braver now that they're not six ales deep and about to piss themselves," Magnus mused.

"Are you sure they need to be taken all the way to camp?" Vassago asked, full mouth turned down in a frown. "Seems like a wasted trip. Nobody will miss them, but I could use a nice day flight." He rotated his shoulders, loosening up the muscles around where his wings would emerge from.

"A swift death is too kind," Magnus replied. "They should be on the right side of some hard labor for a while, I think, since taking advantage of others has been such a point of pride in their current employment."

I shivered again, unused to seeing this colder side of him. I still wasn't afraid of him though, which made me wonder what that said about me.

"Very well. How about now, boys? Are you ready to apologize to the lady?" The white-haired demon raised his blade menacingly.

They shifted on their knees, none of them brave enough to look me in the eye save a few shameful glances.

"*Apologize.*" Magnus's voice was a low, thunderous threat. He somehow managed to use intense volume without shouting.

There was a disjointed chorus of halfhearted apologies. My fingers rose to the grooves in my face. Calla had been recovered, and my vanity was inconsequential. But them simply saying "I'm sorry" would never be enough to fix me. What happened couldn't be changed.

It wasn't enough.

All the rage I'd bottled up for months, the fear, the regret ... all of it bubbled up in a hot sludge. I swallowed the taste of bile, trembling where I stood. Magnus stiffened, effortlessly holding the men still as I released everything I'd held back. Worry, panic, anger ... it all poured out of me in a rush.

I moved outside of myself, fingers raking across their cheeks as vicious claws while I screamed from somewhere deep in my chest. I was no fighter, but my fists flew in solid punches, and I kicked out my feet with all my might. Face, chest, stomach ... it was all fair game. I wanted them to know how badly they'd hurt me and wanted to avenge anyone else they'd treated the same way. I wanted them to feel it all. The solid flesh of their bodies giving way under my rage simultaneously left me satisfied and horrified.

In the end, they all begged for mercy. I hated that it brought me joy.

When I was finished, they all carried my marks on top of their existing injuries—deep scratches on their faces, inflamed patches where bruises were quickly forming, missing teeth, fresh trickles of blood.

Chest heaving, my exhalations a raspy rattle, I stepped back. Magnus's face held respect, empathy. None of the men moved beyond the effort it took to draw breath and wheeze through their pain. I looked down at my stained hands, shocked at what I'd done.

"My lady," Vassago said with a bow, taking hold of one of the men. Magnus directed the other two with a shove toward the iron gate.

I stumbled into the building. I surged hot, then cold; black spots danced in front of my eyes. I couldn't believe I'd done that. Hurt someone like that. It felt so wrong now that it was over. In the moment, however ...

I gagged, rushing through the dining room.

Once safely in the kitchen, I leaned over the sink as the temperature surges washed over me and I fought to keep the contents of my stomach down. When the nausea passed, I scrubbed at my hands with steaming water, the harsh dish soap, and a brush. I didn't stop until I was certain there were no traces of blood or gore left from the men and my skin was red and chapped. My knees started to wobble, so I grabbed a towel and sat myself down on the floor until the urge to vomit passed again.

I knew what those men had done to me. It was mild compared to what others had suffered, I was certain. I was tossed about carelessly while drugged, hurled to a dirty floor, and allowed to be bruised. Cut. But I was not abused like I could have been. My face was damaged, but my body was still my own. I wasn't sure what they'd perpetrated upon me was enough for the punishment Magnus was meting out to them.

Which meant they'd done far worse to many more people, and if that were true, then they deserved what they got. Magnus was not unfair or rash. He didn't arbitrarily dole out severe punishments or beatings. But I couldn't help but feel bad, because they were still just people trying to do a job. To get through life. I was torn, my desire to be empathetic at war with my need for justice.

Magnus found me on the floor, teary-eyed and floating between reality and the strange dreamlike place that the rational part of me knew was shock. "I'm sorry, Grace. I didn't ..." He frowned, mouth pinched, as he brushed his fingertips delicately across my cheek. "I should have handled that differently. Let's get you upstairs." He picked me up as though I were weightless, cradling me in his arms as he mounted the stairs and let himself into my apartment.

Magnus fussed with my pillows, fluffing them while he murmured encouraging platitudes at me. He apologized for bringing them to me, explained that he thought I'd want to see for myself that they were no longer a concern. He brought me water, a plate of snacks, and a pot of tea. He promised to come back as quickly as he could and said he'd ask Vassago to check on me a bit later if he couldn't himself.

I curled up into my blanket after he was gone, searching for the peace I'd promised myself I would feel once those men were finally located. But even as I drifted off to sleep peace was nowhere to be found.

CHAPTER 10
MAGNUS

GRACE WAS NOTHING if not resilient.

After we returned to the collegium, Vassago's guest arrived and Grace rallied, her nap restoring her so well it was like nothing had occurred at all. Guilt had gnawed at me the whole flight over her reaction to the gift I'd so arrogantly presented her with. I should have known a soul geared toward caretaking like hers had no experience with such things. While the depth of her rage had impressed me, I wished I'd done everything differently. Especially now that she was back to pretending everything was fine, that things were like they were before.

It wasn't, and they weren't.

If I had any say about it, they'd never go back again.

As an apology, I made plans that would get us both away from the city, if only for an evening. I'd gone to gather supplies and was just leaving the blacksmith's when Gaius and Caster crossed my path.

Impulse leading me, I approached them. "Caster, I'd like to have a word."

His eyebrow inched up curiously. "Your kind often does. Come to my office?"

I followed him down the street and Gaius fell into step beside me, both of us a few paces behind the loan shark.

"Odd seeing you here, General," Gaius prompted.

"I could say the same, *General*."

If he wanted to play the rank game, I was more than happy to oblige.

Caster gestured for me to lead the way through his grimy office. I took note of the young faces that blinked in surprise when they saw me come through the door. Four of our newest recruits, a disappointing confirmation of what Grace had told me she'd seen.

I followed Caster into his smoke-stained office. Gaius joined us, taking a seat on the sofa off to the side. I remained standing as the loan shark dropped into the aged leather chair behind the worn desk.

"What can I do for you?" Caster asked as I closed the door behind us.

"I need to settle a debt."

"Oh?" His bushy eyebrow raised. "You have no business with me, stone kin. Whose debt might you be covering?"

"Jardin. The entire balance. And I'll take back any collateral you're holding as well." Gaius grunted. "Is there a problem?" I asked, skin prickling from his rapt glare.

Caster laughed, the sound somehow oily. "Gaius here holds a torch for Miss Jardin, I think."

My nostrils flared as testosterone filled the air. "That's unfortunate for him."

"Indeed. And how will you be paying this substantial sum?"

I dropped the pouch of coins on his desk. It had been easy enough to raid one of my troves for the necessary funds, but Caster looked as though he might start crying with joy from the sudden windfall of gold.

"The debt gets cleared, and the family is permanently removed from your books. You'll refuse their business if they come to you in the future."

"Yes, yes." He counted hastily, then started again. "This'll do fine," he muttered, opening a drawer in his desk. He dug around for a moment, then produced a necklace and a ring.

"Mark the books," I demanded, not interested in leaving anything to chance where he was concerned. When he didn't move to do as such I leaned forward and gripped the collar of his shirt, pulling him toward me. "Mark. The. Books."

Gaius continued to burn holes into me with his eyes, shifting around as though spoiling for a fight. I'd be more than happy to oblige, I just wanted this done first.

"No need for that." Caster glared at me, straightening his shirt with a snap once I let go. "I'd hate for there to be bloodshed in my office." He threw a look over at Gaius who grinned at me as though he'd love nothing more than to paint the room red.

Caster took out the ledger and drew a solid black line through the pages with Grace's father's name on them.

It was done.

"Happy now?"

"Not hardly. But you follow through, leave them alone from here on and we have no problem."

"You have my word," he promised. "We're finished here," Caster muttered, going back in to count the coins a third time.

"My thanks," I said, snatching up the jewelry and spinning on my heel.

Gaius came after me, the frustration boiling off his skin as he escorted me outside. All the young men had vanished to somewhere else, likely afraid of being turned in to their respective command.

"She was nearly within my reach," he spat, squaring up in front of me. "I was going to swoop in with the same gesture you just stole out from under me."

A rattle in my chest followed the knot of anger taking root. "She would not have thanked you for it," I insisted, bracing myself for the fight I knew was coming.

People were watching us, gathering around doorways to see what was going to happen between the two large men having a noisy disagreement in the street for all to see.

"No? Seems an immense relief to gift her after watching her scramble to make payments all this time."

I flinched. That he knew something about her that I didn't rankled. That he'd watched her struggle, knowing he could have done something sooner and was only waiting until she was at her most vulnerable made me unspeakably angry.

"She won't thank *me* for doing it either," I clarified through gritted teeth. "She's proud. As she should be."

"You think I don't know that?" he barked the words, darting forward with this fist aimed at my nose. I dodged out of the way, my feet in motion as he started to circle. "I've spent time in your archmage's beloved observatory. Eaten her food, been cared for by her hand. I understand who and how she is. I know what I want when I see it."

My blood began to boil. I returned the punch, landing a glancing blow to his ear as he ducked. "Then you'll also know she isn't interested in you," I snarled. "And she is certainly not an object to be claimed."

"Why, because she'd prefer *you*?" Gaius chuckled, striking out several times in succession. I took a fist to the jaw, but only at partial power due to how quickly we were both moving.

"She is my soul mate, Gaius," I said, landing a solid punch to his nose thanks to his shock. Blood sprayed across his cheek, but he didn't so much as flinch.

"You're lying!"

"I'm not." I had a love-hate relationship with the words I said next. "I've already claimed her."

His fists fell to his sides, the fight leaking out of him abruptly. My old comrade was not himself, not by a long shot.

"You had a revered stone kin warrior for a wife, all those years. Your fated mate, correct? As a pair you produced many children. And now you get the cook as a soul mate as well?" His face crumpled in disgust.

Guilt prickled. I knew it wasn't fair. Gaius had never mated, not in hundreds of years. I'd never known him to be lonely nor jealous. But it seemed there was plenty about him I didn't know … or simply hadn't noticed.

I could easily understand feeling slighted over the situation. I knew how rare it was for me to have been gifted both. Grace was unexpected but so very welcome, and that irritated him to the point of throwing another swing at my face when I asked, "Are you well, Gaius?"

"I'm *fine*." He struck out, glancing a hit off my temple, but I was able to dance out of his reach.

"You don't seem like it. You are acting out of sorts. We don't treat women the way you just described Grace. Like an object to be obtained. To be bought off after being left to toil only to suffer further under a new master. Women are honored and revered by our kind, yes? Not to mention the fact that you're a stone kin general moonlighting as a criminal's personal bodyguard. For what? Money? For fun? It is not logical. It is beneath you, Gaius."

We both stopped moving as he sagged, shaking his head. The crowd that had gathered dispersed quickly when he started to make eye contact with the gawkers. "I did not intend to treat her that way. I would have been kind to her. Generous."

"Nothing was stopping you from doing that from the start."

His eye twitched, and I knew I'd hit my mark. "We all have our roles to play," Gaius said calmly, swiping the blood from below his nose with the side of his hand. "Don't you agree, General?"

Ice surged through my veins, cooling my anger. "What's that supposed to mean, Gaius? Speak plainly."

"It's just that we all have certain paths to walk in order to accomplish the tasks set forth for us by those in control. Those with the power. I'm sure you know that as well as I do."

"As a general, you *are* the one in power. You get to choose many things."

"This is true. And as such, there are a multitude of others that are out of my hands. I am doing my *job*, as you are." He emphasized the word intently, and I understood. He was either undercover working for Caster or doing a very good job of pretending that was the case. "Besides, we do not all have an archmage with other special abilities in our back pocket to wield against the enemy."

I stared at him, seeing traces of weariness in his features for the first time. I did know that we all played our part, but the cryptic way he discussed such things made me wary. And I didn't appreciate the way he spoke of Rylan, though I understood some of the bitterness. There were many of our kind who still thought of him as the enemy, just another demon to be destroyed like the troublesome lower-level hordes that were our common foe.

"It doesn't have to be us against each other," I suggested. "That only benefits them." I wasn't even certain who *they* were, but I could guess it was someone on the council.

It was too uncomfortable to think that it was the council as a whole, but I couldn't rule out that possibility either. I was beginning to see many things they were responsible for that didn't line up with the rhetoric they loved to spew. "What would happen if I reported you and those boys to the council?" I asked.

"It would be a complete waste of your time to report something they have duly sanctioned."

I stiffened. They were planted intentionally then. I no longer believed I could fully trust a soul who held a seat at the council table if that were true.

Gaius, looking defeated, stared off into the distance.

"I'm here," I offered. "When you're ready to talk. The observatory is always open to you. To them." I waved an arm in the vague direction of the Collegium d'Arcan. "There are many things we could come to an agreement about, I think."

For centuries, we'd known one another. All that time I'd thought we were much the same. I was beginning to see that we didn't really know each other at all. It was a realization that left me thoroughly discomforted. Too many things had gone unnoticed for too many years.

"You should set that nose," I smirked. "It's gone more crooked than normal."

"Fuck off." His mouth twitched, and he crossed his arms to stop himself from doing just that.

"Fair enough. My offer stands."

He gave a short nod before stomping back into Caster's shoddy office.

I patted the pocket where I'd shoved Grace's jewelry, ensuring it was still where it should be before starting off toward the vendors I'd originally intended to visit.

My afternoon may have taken an abrupt turn, but I had plans to complete. I'd be damned if a little political strife and a fistfight with an old comrade would derail me.

CHAPTER 11
GRACE

"WHAT?" MY HANDS tingled as adrenaline surged through my body. Surely, he hadn't been so bold. I almost certainly had misunderstood what he'd said. I had to have.

Magnus sat at the round dining table casually, as though he didn't have a care in the world. He was wearing the green linen shirt that brought out his eyes best and black suede pants. He looked like walking lust.

But he sat there like he hadn't just dropped a bomb between us as I reeled. "The debt has been paid. You're never to go back there again. Promise me." He slid the jewelry across the table toward me, the metal grating softly against the wood.

Emotions warred under my skin. Naturally, unbridled rage presented first. I flushed hot as I picked up my necklace and my mother's ring. "You had no cause to do that. Nor any right to tell me where I will and will not go. I'm a grown woman and can make my own decisions in that regard, thank you."

"I know full well how capable you are, Grace. I meant no insult."

His voice was low and soft, acceptance in his eyes for whatever vitriol I spewed his direction.

"Could have fooled me," I sniped. "We were doing just fine, I was all set to make the payment next week—"

"And now you don't have to. I take care of what's mine, Grace." His tone was firm, a layer of heat coating the last.

"I never asked you to do this." My hands trembled as adrenaline rushed through my veins. He inhaled deeply, nostrils flaring as he calmed himself down. I was baiting him. I was downright *spoiling* for a fight, and the fact that he wasn't falling for it infuriated me further.

"Your parents can finally enjoy their retirement. You can stop worrying yourself sick over it all. No more doing things like picking up shifts at the beer garden, though we both know that was a double-edged plan from the beginning."

"It wasn't your problem to solve." My voice caught as the threat of tears tightened my throat.

His mouth ticked as he flinched from the change in my emotion. "No, but it was something I could easily do to help you. So I did."

"How dare you ... *insert* yourself where you were asked not to interfere. In fact, I remember telling you quite clearly to stay out of my business." Emotions collided messily in my chest, I leaned over and slapped him across the face. Immediately, I gasped, shocked I'd done it. My hand tingled, and while his face had turned to the side with my blow, his expression remained the same neutral it had been as he shifted it right back.

"I did it knowing you might hate me for it. It was the only option." He laced his fingers together on the table, his whole being still and serene. While everything in me rioted, he sat there calmly. Just watching. It was maddening.

"I do," I said, but there was no heat behind my words. "I do hate you for it." Even as I said it, I knew it was a lie. Relief surged through me, a cascade of warmth in my veins and realizations that I could finally relax.

"I accept that," he repeated, but he didn't move. He knew it was a lie too.

I slid into the chair, head spinning as I stared at the jewelry. "I'll pay you back," I muttered, furious that there were tears in my eyes as I looked up at him. "Every cent."

"I'm not interested in your money, Grace. Nor your father's. I did this because I wanted to, not because I wanted to assume your debt and simply be a kinder usurer you owe." His eyebrows slanted down, his mouth pursed as though he'd eaten something sour.

"I cannot owe you, Magnus. I don't wish to owe *anyone*. Rylan skirts the issue by claiming the rent he sends for my parents is an arrangement that's simply a benefit of my employment. But it's still a gift that weighs on my conscience."

"You'll have to take that up with him. I don't have any involvement with those affairs. But as far as I'm concerned, you owe me nothing now and never will. Not for that. It's just money. More will come in, and more will go out. It is inconsequential in the grand scheme of the tides of time. But your happiness? Your freedom? Those are worth a value greater than measure."

Inside, I was screaming, willing him to understand, but I was also grateful that he was ready to face my wrath over such a thing and a melted puddle because of his sweet words.

"*Just* money?" I scolded. "Only those with too much coin and too little sense speak of it so casually."

The corner of his mouth twitched, his effort at fighting a smile nearly lost. Had he done so, or laughed at me, I would have lost all control of my temper. "Perhaps. You're welcome to be angry about that as well, if you need to be. I can bear it all, Grace, whatever you need me to carry, I can manage."

A long silence fell between us. Internally, I unraveled cell by cell, my panic only enhanced by his patient, understanding silence. I had to try three times before words would form again. "Thank you," I finally grated out.

His eyebrows shot up, shock taking the place of frustration on his handsome features. "What?"

"You heard me. Please don't make me repeat it."

The battle I'd been fighting was lost. Relief and gratitude won out over anger by a long shot. The edges of my mother's ring pressed into my cheek as I sobbed into my hands.

"Grace." I heard Magnus's chair scrape angrily against the floor, then his warmth wrapped around me as he hugged me to his chest. He let me get it all out, a solid presence as I cried into his shoulder while his hand stroked my hair.

"I'm sorry," I apologized, mortified I'd cried at all but especially all over him.

"I'm not." He wiped at my face with his broad thumbs, removing the remnants of my tears. "Though I will say, I was mightily prepared for a tongue lashing, not crying. The tears are much more terrifying."

I choked out a wet laugh. "Why do you have to be so kind?" I complained half-heartedly.

"It's a curse, truly."

I swiped at my eyes again, the laughter pushing a few rogue tears out. "It would be much easier if you weren't so detestably nice. Handsome. Strong." His chest puffed out as I continued. "Shame you're so full of yourself, though it does balance some things out."

He held his breath for a beat but then chuckled. "There you are, feisty Little Rabbit. Come. Let me make you dinner for a change."

I took his hand, feeling wildly irresponsible for leaving the collegium again, though I had no duty to stay. Once we were in the yard, Magnus scooped me up against his body.

"Up you go," he said before pressing his mouth to mine as he squatted down to grab my thighs. He situated my legs around his waist and my arms around his neck to his liking, all without breaking the kiss.

"Wait. What are you—" Launching into flight from standing stock-still was absolutely terrifying. I screamed into the stout muscles of his chest as Magnus's powerful wings lifted us high into the sky.

His arms kept me banded safely against his body as he carried me over the dense forest. My heart fluttered fiercely behind my ribs, the wind tangling in my hair as we moved above the trees. The heavy beat of his wings, the way the air responded to him … it was so effortless and foreign I could barely wrap my thoughts around what was happening.

I'd never traveled this direction before, especially not so deep into the woods as he was taking us. My heart thudded against my ribs, a flash of anxiety taking root. I breathed over it, however. Magnus wouldn't hurt me. I had to trust in that.

When he finally made his descent, I was thankful. My ears and nose were icy, and I needed a moment to collect my thoughts with my feet solidly on the ground.

He landed us in a small grassy clearing in front of a round wooden hut.

"What is this place?" I asked, swaying as gravity owned me once again.

Magnus opened the door and gestured for me to enter in front of him.

"This is one of our way stations. There are a few scattered throughout the city and the area beyond. If we're too far from an encampment, we can use a station for food, shelter, clothing … whatever is needed."

My eyes brushed over the simple decor and sturdy furniture. There was a small but very functional kitchen with something fragrantly savory cooking in the oven. To one side, there was a large bed near a lit fireplace, and close to the door sat a small dining table. I guessed there was a bathroom as well, but couldn't see it from where I stood.

"Is someone else here?"

He frowned. "No. Why?"

"Because a fire's lit and there's food cooking," I said, eyes narrowed at him.

"Yes, because I left them like that before coming to fetch you."

"*Fetch* me?" Blood stirring again, I balked at the notion that the evening had all been an elaborate setup.

Magnus inhaled slowly, setting his heavy hands on my shoulders. "Yes. I planned to bring you here tonight well before I happened upon Gaius and Caster in the city. I saw them while I was buying the supplies for this meal." He walked me backwards until my knees hit the side of the mattress and I was forced to sit. "You and I having a quiet evening to ourselves was always the plan, Grace." I was distracted by him dropping to his knees. It put him nearly eye level with me for a change. "Running into them was simply good fortune. I took advantage of the opportunity."

"You paid my debt because the opportunity presented itself?" Something about that didn't sit quite right.

"Yes. Though I would have done it anyway."

I stiffened, but he was undeterred, placid as a still lake as he carefully unlaced and removed my boots. "Knowing how I felt about it?"

"Yes."

I didn't know whether to be impressed or angry. "Why?"

As my second boot came off, he sat back on his heels, hands flat on his broad thighs. "Because, Grace. As I said, I take care of what's mine."

"And I'm yours?"

He grunted, hands teasing up my legs, my skirt traveling upward with his nimble fingers. "Damn right. You know you are."

Breathing suddenly seemed difficult, heavy. His warm hands roved stealthily on as he lifted up, balanced on his knees. "And you're mine?" I asked, voice frustratingly breathy. I couldn't think when his hands were on me like that.

"As long as you'll have me." He growled low, fisting my skirt as he pushed it above my waist.

"Are you distracting me on purpose?" I asked.

With his palm flat against my chest, he pushed me gently backwards. My body sank into the blankets and soft mattress as he pulled off my undergarments. The fabric whispered down my legs as he pressed kisses all along the inside of one thigh, then the other.

"Is it working?" he asked, voice low and rumbly against my skin.

I shivered, able only to breathe out as his tongue swiped the damp length of me. "Maybe."

"Mmm. I'll have to try harder then." He worked me in earnest then, feasting on my flesh with teeth and tongue. I couldn't do anything but relax into his firm grip as his mouth lashed at me and his arm held me in place, firmly settled across my hips.

"Magnus," I whined, trying to back away as he focused solely on sucking at my clit, one of his thick fingers gently probing my entrance.

"I'm not moving until you come at least twice."

Heat bloomed in my blood as the endorphins rushed around and the pressure built low in my abdomen. This man and his dirty mouth were going to be the end of me. I'd gone years and years without so much as a glance of attention, but he'd made me as wanton as a teenager just discovering the joys of the flesh.

He curved his finger upwards, pressing into that soft spot that always made me see stars. The pressure relaxed on my clit, and he traded for slow licks with his tongue instead, making my thighs quake. The rumble of his growl pushed me right up against the edge of climax.

When he used his teeth, I was done for. I plunged into ecstasy, bucking against his mouth as he continued his ministrations. "I can't—" I protested, unsure what I even wanted to say.

He pulled away from me with a wet noise, though his finger never stopped curling into that spot. "We've been over this, Little Rabbit. You can. And you will. Just one more. For now."

I moaned as his hot mouth returned to my sensitive flesh, lathing and sucking and consuming me whole. He was a perceptive lover, adjusting one little thing if he noticed me twitch or moan, and it led to me being an over-sensitized throbbing mess. I reached down and threaded my fingers through his thick curls, my grip pulling him further into me which apparently was all it took.

Another climax surged through my body, leaving me burning from my toes to the roots of my hair. "Saints," I cursed, panting as I stared at the ceiling, thighs shaking as he gave one final long lick.

He smirked as he wiped his mouth on the back of his hand, leaving me in a puddle on the bed. "I did promise to make you dinner, did I not?"

"What?"

"You're the best meal I've had in ages, Grace."

CHAPTER 12
MAGNUS

"VERY CLEVER," GRACE admonished, her voice still heavy.

I loved the look of her on that bed, disheveled and flushed in places only I got to see. Her shallow breaths gave me life, and the feel of her body tensing against mine turned me into nothing more than a man with a singular goal. My sole mission became to give her as much pleasure as possible, for as long as possible. Nothing else mattered. I could disappear into her for days, given the opportunity. It was dangerous, but I loved every moment of it.

"Though I imagine you're hungry too?" I asked, the taste of her ripe on my tongue.

She sat up on her elbows. "You're not going to ... finish what you started?"

"I most certainly did. Twice, if I was paying attention correctly."

She scoffed, the scowl I loved so much back on her face. "You know what I mean."

The ache in my pants was definitely interested in what she was asking about, but it would wait. I had more plans, and I didn't want dinner to burn.

"Soon, Little Rabbit. Let's get you fed. I spent an unreasonable amount of time making this, I'd hate to see it wasted."

I went into the kitchen, Grace a few steps behind. "What've you made?"

Steam slapped me in the face as I opened the oven door and pulled out the casserole. "Nothing fancy, but I always did love my mother's cottage pie. As we're in a little cottage, I thought …" I shrugged, turning to a pile of mush at her soft features smiling over at me.

"Well, it smells lovely."

I dished us up and served her, scrounging up a bottle of wine from one of the cabinets.

"It's delicious." She beamed at me, her hair wild around her face as she tasted it.

"That's a high compliment," I preened, unable to disguise my pride in having pulled off the meal as well as having impressed her.

We ate in silence for a while, sharing warm glances across the table. We'd fallen into that strange zone again, that awkward place between how we existed in the daylight and how we behaved in bed.

"Eat up," I encouraged. "You'll need your energy."

Her eyebrows went up in question, but she did as instructed.

A short time later, with plates cleaned and the fire well stoked, I invited her outside to look at the abundance of stars in the sky.

"It's so dark out here. And quiet." She rubbed her arms, the evening chill abrupt after the warmth of the cabin. "Can you show me where we are in relation to the city?" she asked.

I held her hand in mine, pointing with her finger at her landmarks.

"This is d'Arcan," I turned her to the side, back the way we'd come. "That is the city center," I adjusted her a bit to the left.

"Over there is the Dread Forest and the main road through the mountains to the granite valley."

"What's around us here?"

I shook my head. "A whole lot of nothing."

"So the chances of me running into someone in the trees ...?"

My pulse thudded heavily in my veins. "Zero."

A mischievous smile spread across Grace's mouth as she turned around, gauging her best route through the trees, her skirt already fisted in her hands.

"If you run, Little Rabbit, I will chase."

"I'd be terribly disappointed if you didn't." She darted forward, stealing a quick kiss before dashing past me into the trees.

I was hard already but forced myself to count to ten before following after her.

The sound of her breaking branches and stomping through the soft underbrush guided me as I took a few steps into the trees to get my bearings before truly giving chase. While I focused on breathing and counting, I loosened the lacings on my clothing.

Closing my eyes, I let my stone skin slip over me. My wings tucked in tight, but still a solid presence at my back, I breathed in and listened to the way her movement echoed through the quiet night. Her sweet honey scent lingered on one of the nearest trees, as though she'd pressed a hand to it in passing.

"Run, Little Rabbit," I grumbled, blood pumping hot in my veins as I gave over to the parts of me that wanted to become nothing more than a predator. She would be the sweetest prey I'd ever pursued, I was sure of it.

I moved faster, scenting her on the greenery. I found a hair over a branch, a droplet of blood on a thorny vine. Every crackle and snap propelled me in her direction. It was pure frustration at the idea of her becoming injured and the musical sound of her laughter that kept me mostly myself, even with the need to hunt riding my senses.

She was doing a terrible job keeping quiet or confusing her trail. We'd have to have some proper lessons so she could improve her skills, then we could both enjoy this game all the more.

I moved faster, my wings buffeting the wind in a way that allowed me to glide. I was sure she had gone down the path that had broken through the trees thanks to her smell and the silence of all wildlife giving her away. She'd gone quiet, but I felt her essence as I traveled down the trail at full speed. As the flat dirt gave way to a shallow hill, I skidded to a stop, sniffing around me.

A newer-growth sapling had taken the brunt of my stop and was now bent at the middle. I took a moment to repair the damage I'd caused while opening my senses to the area around me.

She was gone.

The clever little kitchen witch had doubled back on me.

With a broad grin and blood pumping through my veins burning hot with desire, I charged back the way I came, careful to watch for any sign of her passing through. Threads from her skirt and a clear foot imprint gave away the spot where she'd tried to leap over some low bushes, though they were barely a thought for me to hurdle.

I was satisfied with a surprised squeak as she burst from a crouch behind a small rock outcropping as I approached. "Clever, Little Rabbit," I said, her eyes glossy and her smile wide as I crowded her into the trunk of a tree. "But not fast enough."

Chest heaving, she moaned as I devoured her with a kiss. My hands tangled in her hair while the length of her body pressed against mine as I took everything she had to give. She lashed back at me, nipping at my lips and clawing her hands down my arms. Where I ended and she began was inconsequential. I breathed her in, tasted her as thoroughly as I could before finally letting her go so I could get even closer.

She dropped to her knees the moment I pulled away, her hands working at the laces on my trousers with expert precision.

"Grace," I growled.

"I want to," she said, wrapping a hand around my cock. She tentatively circled the sensitive head with her tongue, looking up at me for my reaction. I exhaled through my nose, sensation rioting under my skin.

I tangled a hand in her hair, which she must have accepted as a signal of approval, then her warm, soft mouth was around me and all rational thought fled. Grace twirled her tongue over the crown again, then took me deeper into her mouth. She applied both hands, stacked one on top of the other, and twisted them in separate directions as she bobbed her mouth over as much of me as she could take and still breathe.

I made the mistake of looking down to see those wide, hazel eyes peering back up at me. The familiar tingle of impending release exploded near my spine, and her tongue lapping at the droplets of moisture it produced nearly pushed me over the edge. Her hands dropped away, and she gripped back of my thighs as she opened wider, taking me deep into her throat. My head fell back, eyes unfocused as they took in the stars above me, then more exploded behind them.

"Grace," I warned, but she was encouraged by the strain in my voice instead of deterred. Her speed increased, one hand returning as I abandoned all hope of regaining control. My climax swept through me a roar leaving my throat as I came down hers, fingers tangled in her curls.

When I had regained some balance, I tried to pull her up by her hands, but instead, we ended up in the soft leaves with me on my back and her sprawled over my chest.

"You're a gift, Little Rabbit," I breathed, reveling in the soft quality her eyes took on just before I meshed my mouth with hers again.

Our kisses were slower, more about discovery than passion as we lay on the ground. I turned my body, rolling her off me and then under me as she clung to my shoulders. I breathed in her sweet scent, pressed my mouth to that soft place where her jaw met her ear, then traveled down the column of her neck. My teeth nipped at her collarbone, and she arched up into me. I took my time. I tasted and touched and planned the next fifteen interludes I wanted to have with her.

She was beautiful, leaves tangled in her hair, dirt smudges on her face and arms. I pulled her back to her feet and danced her backward toward the rocks.

"Pull your skirt up." I turned her so she was on her stomach, her feet barely touching the ground as I positioned her to the right height. Slipping her underthings down to her ankles, I gripped one round globe in each hand. She glistened between her legs, proof that I wasn't alone in my desire. "Hang on, Little Rabbit."

I sank into her slowly after giving my cock a firm grip and tug with my hand. The sound she made sent a tingle into my chest, and I feasted on every single one of her moans as I pumped into her from behind. She stretched around me, a perfect fit just like the time before. I'd never get enough of her.

My stamina should've been better, but when she started to press her ass back into me, I knew I was in trouble. I could feel myself hitting the end of her as she took all of me, her inner muscles fluttering against my shaft as I rubbed on a spot she liked. Grace was no passive lover, canting her hips and moving one of her legs to better balance ... even putting her hand between her legs to rub at her clit to speed things along.

I was doomed.

"Faster," she gasped.

I complied, holding on to her hips with what I feared was a bruising grip as I thrust myself as fast and deep as I could.

"Magnus."

"Yes, Little Rabbit?"

"Don't stop. I'm so close …" She breathed out heavily, and I felt her body let go. I tensed but kept going, pushing her through the peak. I pressed myself in as deep as I could go as her legs trembled and she cried out, and my cock throbbed in response.

When she could breathe again, I continued, rocking in and out slowly as the heavy tingle chased up my spine. Grace whimpered, and I couldn't take anymore. My climax left me pulsing inside her as she clutched at the rock with her fingertips.

"Well done, Grace." I sighed, catching her in my arms as she slid bonelessly away from the rocks.

Well done, indeed.

CHAPTER 13

GRACE

I WAS GRATEFUL FOR the warm fire we'd left burning and how close my bed for the night was by the time Magnus carried me back to the hut. My body was sore in the most delicious of ways, but I was ready for some coziness. A hot bath, a snack, and a serious night's sleep all sounded heavenly.

I stared at the strange contraption that was nothing more than a drain in the middle of a stone floor with a sprayer head attached to some piping.

"What is that?" I looked at him, perplexed.

"A shower," he said simply. "You've never used one?"

"No. Where's the tub?"

He chuckled. "Well, it seems there are some innovations the stone kin can claim yet. No tub. We're too big, and it takes too much time to fill—we get impatient. This sprays down on you like concentrated rain. Hot water of course, but no soaking in your own debris once you start washing. It just goes down into a drain under the hut and a distance away before filtering into the soil."

"That's ..." I had nothing further to say. My head tilted to the side as I considered how that would work.

A true gentleman despite his laughter, Magnus switched on the water so it would run as hot as possible, ducked under the forceful spray, then stuck a hand out for me. "Come on, Little Rabbit. You'll be fine."

My skepticism about the plumbing was exceptionally short lived. The hot spray was dreamy as it sluiced over my body and through my hair. Magnus efficiently plucked the leaves and debris from my hair before scrubbing it with some very fragrant shampoo. Then he took the same care to remove all the dirt from my flesh.

He stood outside the warm spray, where I'd no doubt be shivering, water droplets running down his tanned chest, muscles rolling hypnotically under his skin as he lavished me with his gentle ministrations. While Magnus washed me, his touch was intimate but not incendiary. There was no part of me he didn't ensure was clean, and the multitude of aches and pains I'd acquired were all accounted for under his fingertips.

Perhaps we both needed a moment to breathe after the result of our chase.

Once we were both clean, he wrapped me in a towel and took me off to the bed, tucking me under the puffy blankets as he gathered up enough food for a whole other meal. There'd been a lovely suspended reality quality to our time in the forest, and the hut was no different. It was dark outside, but the lack of distinction left it a mystery whether it was simply evening or the middle of the night.

The fire crackled low as he sat with his back propped against the iron footboard, facing me. His legs were crossed, a platter of items on the coverlet between us.

"Do you cook often?"

He shook his head. "I get by but no. I'm so rarely in the same place for long stretches I've gotten quite used to relying on others to take care of my meals. Present company being my absolute favorite option, of course."

"No need for that kind of flattery, I'm already in your bed," I teased. "But truly, you're good at it. I'm sure you have a treasure trove of recipes for things I've never heard of. Maybe we could come to an arrangement?"

"I like the sound of that," he rumbled.

Heaviness settled in my limbs, a peaceful exhaustion weighed me down as I sampled the snacks and sipped at my wine.

"Ygritte was always the cook," Magnus said, looking off into the fire nostalgically, "but my son Coltor is the most dedicated chef in our family. He can take field rations and turn them into gourmet meals. It's baffling."

I couldn't help but smile. This was the part of Magnus I adored most. He was clearly completely dedicated to his children. "Will they be coming to the city again soon?"

He grinned broadly. "Yes, I believe so. My girls were quite taken with Calla. They love the idea of a new cousin to teach stone kin things to."

"And the boys?"

"I hope so. Their assignments will all be terming out soon. It's been quite some time since we were all together for longer than a few days."

My mind wandered to a place I hadn't expected, where I worried about what his children would think of me. Of the fact that their father had taken a new woman into his bed. I worried how they might feel about me not just being human but also decades younger than any of them. It was an awkward feeling, and my stomach twisted.

"Grace?" Magnus asked softly. "Where did you go, Little Rabbit? Have I said something wrong?"

"No." I shook my head. "Why?"

"You're frowning. Intensely."

"Am I?" I touched my chin with my fingertips, focused on the concern in his eyes. "I was thinking about your children," I admitted. "What they might think of ... this." I gestured between us.

Magnus reached out and took my hand into his. "It's none of their concern," he said solemnly. "But I'd like to think they'd be happy for me. For you. It's not every day that one finds a soul mate."

I blinked at the word. "Is that what I am?"

"Yes," he answered. No hesitation. No doubt.

"How do you know?"

Magnus slid off the bed, hastily clearing the dishes. When he returned, he cuddled in close to my side. My head rested in the divot where his chest and shoulder met, his heartbeat loud and strong under my ear.

"I feel it," he said finally. "That sounds overly simple, but it's true. You're imbedded in my soul, Grace. My heart knows when you're near. It beats differently than it did before it recognized you as belonging to me. Do you feel it?"

I closed my eyes, the sentiment in his words overwhelming me. My own heart squeezed in response. "Not like that, but yes."

"Describe it to me."

"It's like an ache but not. I can feel when you're in the building, I think. When you leave, I worry. It's like a switch goes off." I frowned, realizing the truth in my own words. Magnus nuzzled into my hair, planting a soft kiss before resting his cheek on my head. "Is this like Rylan and Calla?"

"Sort of. They are fated, which is much more intense. Some fated couples can hear one another speak in their minds, feel what the other feels ... it can be overwhelming."

"You were fated with your wife?"

"Yes." I heard the caution he used in his tone. I appreciated that he was trying to protect my feelings, but I was too curious not to ask. We all had a past. It was part of us, but not the only one.

"Do you miss her?"

Magnus exhaled through his nose. "In many ways, yes. She was my partner for a very long time. I may always miss her. Always love her. I grieved ... well, let's just say my mourning period was concerningly long, but I have fully grieved her passing. I've helped my children work through theirs as well. I have accepted that chapter of my life has closed. She would not begrudge me moving on. We discussed it more than once. It's a hazard of living as long as we do."

"I can't imagine losing someone like that." My heart hurt for him, but I also appreciated the subtle way he let me know I wasn't in competition with her.

"Have you lost someone before, Grace? You're not old enough to be a widow, I don't think? Though as a soldier, perhaps I should know better than to make a statement like that."

I scoffed lightly. "Flattery will get you everywhere. I'm plenty old enough to be a widow." On a long exhale, I admitted, "I was engaged once."

Magnus made an interested noise in his chest and shifted us so we were lying down flat but still cuddled together. Sleep would not be far behind if I allowed myself to close my eyes, but I wasn't ready to give up this stolen night quite yet.

"Tell me. I want to know everything about you, even if it makes me want to commit violence."

I laughed and swatted at his arm. "He's not worth the trouble."

"Clearly, but that doesn't mean my impulse won't react accordingly. Tell me," he prompted again.

My voice was low, a compliment to the hush of the insular hut and our little bed nest. The fire put off just enough heat, and my muscles were lax as I rested against him. It was the worst kind of temptation to lay my soul bare to this man.

"Well before I came to the collegium, one of my father's business associates proposed a match between his son and I." I remembered the boy's face, and it was no better in recall than it had been in real time. "He looked like a cocker spaniel—"

Magnus barked a laugh. "Sorry, sorry. Please continue."

"Well, he did! But I was a good daughter and willing to sacrifice some vanity for a good match. He was sweet, kind ... a bit on the unambitious side, but that was okay. He had a built-in career with his father, and we would have a comfortable life most likely. We dated for several months, and I'll be the first to admit I was quick to indulge my hormones since I thought our marriage was a foregone conclusion."

"Oh my," Magnus grumbled, but I had a feeling he was guessing the next part wrong. Most did.

"No, I didn't get pregnant. In fact, quite the opposite. My mother was not supposed to be able to have children. I came to them very late as a complete surprise. The women in our family have a ... defect. It skips around where it likes, but the issue can be tracked back for several generations. I'm missing my womb altogether, but every one of us has some sort of complication with our reproductive abilities." I paused, the old wound pinching but not hurting like it once had. Magnus's arms pulled me closer.

"When he found out, he called off the engagement. Started a whole lot of trouble by claiming my parents defrauded his father. It led to a split in the partnership, even. It was a very hard time all the way around. I think the debt to Caster started there, honestly."

"That was cruel of him."

"It was, but not unexpected. I was young and naive. It honestly never occurred to me that it would be a problem. When you're young and unmarried, having a baby too soon is the thing you're focused on. It was for the best, anyway. After that, I helped my father at the shop, tried to help my mother with the neighborhood kids ... it worked out."

"I'm sorry he reduced you to your ability to have children, Grace. You have much more to offer the world than that." I smiled, at his sweet words, my eyelids growing heavy. "You're perfect, and I mean that. Your scars are proof of what you've survived. In fact, scars are revered by my people, did you know that?" I opened my eyes to find him peering down at me, sincerity in his eyes. His warm fingertips traced along my cheek and I found myself tearing up. "You're beautiful, Grace. One of the most stunning creatures I've ever seen."

I swallowed over the lump in my throat, trying to communicate through a nod that my tears were not distress. I knew he was telling me the absolute truth. There was no way to avoid sharing one's whole heart in this little cottage, it seemed. Everything was so different than it was in our normal day-to-day life. I wished we didn't have to leave.

"If I'd married the cocker spaniel, then I wouldn't have been able to have this." I finally managed to say as I snuggled deeper into his embrace, exhaustion catching up to me.

"That would have been a shame indeed."

Magnus was worth a hundred times whatever happiness that sham of a marriage would have brought me. I was safe. Cared for. Magnus didn't try to bend me to his whims and listened to what I wanted, all while sparring with me in a way that suited us both.

The truth of our link echoed warmly in my chest as I fell off to sleep.

He was my soul mate.

CHAPTER 14
MAGNUS

I HATED TO WAKE her, but ... "Time to go, Little Rabbit."

"Mmm. Five more minutes?"

She'd be missed if anyone went to get their breakfast and couldn't find her anywhere, but I couldn't deny her a little more time. "I'm going to tidy up, then I'll fly you back."

"Do we have to?" she grumbled, rolling away as I slid off the bed.

"Sadly, yes. We both have work to do."

She muttered something incoherent then flung the covers back before stomping off to the bathroom.

I chuckled as I cleaned up the dishes we'd used and disposed of any food that couldn't be saved. By the time I finished, she'd returned and was busily making the bed.

"Can we come back here?" she asked, looking around fondly as I locked the door behind us.

"As much as you'd like," I promised.

With a curt nod, she reached out for me after I'd shifted. I happily lifted her against me before launching us into the sky. The flight back was not nearly as thrilling as the one out had been.

Grace clung tightly to me, but knowing we were headed back to reality put a bit of a damper on the joy.

When we landed in the yard of the collegium, we had an audience. Vassago was already dressed in his finery and stood with his arms crossed as he spoke to Gaius.

Grace was unusually stone-faced as she met the two men's gazes. "I'll be inside preparing breakfast." She gave Gaius as wide a berth as she could manage and all but jogged into the building.

"Has something happened?" I asked, a pit in my stomach. They were both stern, as though discussing ill news.

"A significant horde has popped up just beyond the edge of the city, in the Dread Forest."

I stiffened, glad for the restful sleep I'd gotten. One of the oldest of our kind, a wily sorceress named Ophelia, kept her home where he was describing. "Ophelia."

"Yes. She is in probable danger. As many soldiers as can be mustered have been called by the council to help fight them." Gaius shifted on his feet. "We were hoping your archmage could join us as well." His mouth twisted at this, as though the words tasted bad.

"I'm happy to join, I just need to get my blade. As for the archmage, he's traveling. I'm not sure the best way to get him a message, but if he can come, I'm sure he will."

Gaius bowed his head in a short nod.

"I'm happy to join you in my brother's absence," Vassago offered. "I could use a good workout."

I cracked a smile at the demon, further amused when Gaius's expression morphed from disbelief to outright shock. There were plenty of rumors that I had befriended a high-level demon or two. But I understood that seeing it in person was a very different scenario. We were creatures designed for and tasked with dispatching all demon kind that ventured earth-side. To have another demon volunteering to help? I'm sure it was a bitter pill to swallow.

"Not everything they say is truth," I reminded him.

"Not half the things they say are," he countered in agreement, quickly composing himself. "Though they'll be glad to hear of your willingness to join. We're rallying at the last gate on the main road."

"We won't be far behind you."

He took off, a cloud of dust swirling in his wake.

"Shall we eat first?"

Vassago nodded, expression closed and thoughtful. "Absolutely. We need to fortify ourselves. It's possible it sounds worse than it is, but ..." He tilted his head to the side.

"It's usually not. Can you get a message to your brother?"

"Yes, I'll go do that now and meet you in the dining room."

Once I'd collected my demon-killing Light blade from my room, I returned to the dining hall. Grace was already prepared for us with tankards of coffee and plates full of food.

"Eat up. I don't need to know the details, but I can tell bad news when I see it." She dusted her hands across her apron and returned to the kitchen.

Vassago raised an eyebrow at me.

"Don't start."

"I said nothing, stone man." He gave me time to begin eating, then added, "But it's about time the two of you finally did something with all that chemistry boiling over between you."

"*About time?*" I mocked. "You just got here, demon."

"I know. And it was already driving me mad, so I can't imagine how relieved everyone else will feel when they find out."

I flicked a drop of hot coffee at his face, which earned me a foul hand gesture.

Grace usually had an innate sense for when people were finished eating and swooped in to take the plates away before we could think about it. When she didn't come back, I gathered them up myself and started for the kitchen.

"I'll be out in the courtyard," Vago said.

I found her eating her own breakfast at the counter with her hair pulled up in a very utilitarian bun. I noticed a few marks from our escapades dotted the back of her neck.

"Do you need anything to take with you?" she asked softly.

"No, but thank you."

"I ..." She gave a self-deprecating smile and shook her head. "I don't know how to do this part either, I guess."

"Which part are we at now, Little Rabbit?"

"The part where you go off to be a soldier and I stay here and pretend I'm not worried about you. The part where people know about us and have questions, but I don't have answers. The part—"

"Grace. Breathe." I set my hands on her shoulders.

After a great big inhale, panic still rested on her face. "I'm not used to feeling like this."

"Like what?"

"Vulnerable."

I pulled her into my arms, squeezed her tightly for a long moment, then released her so I could kiss her lush mouth in hopes of relaxing her a little bit. "We'll figure it out together, okay?"

She breathed again, then nodded. "Okay."

"I've been a soldier for hundreds of years. This is my job, and I'm damn good at it. I'll be fine. Vassago will be with me, and maybe Rylan. Gaius too." She stiffened. "I wouldn't dream of asking you to be his friend, Grace, but I would suggest you be open to the idea that he may be around sometimes. He's going through something, and his affection for you seems to be tangled up in that. I don't believe he ever meant to make you feel uncomfortable, though I know he did. It's up to him to apologize for that, however."

"You'll be fine?"

"Yes, I will." I smiled at her. My fierce Little Rabbit was a whole different person when she was concerned for my well-being instead of threatening it.

"Okay." She nodded enthusiastically, and I saw the change happen on her face—it was fascinating. It was as though she'd managed to grapple her worries into submission and was ready to plow forward with her day. "I'll be right here when you get back," she promised. "I might even plan to have enough food around to feed you a good meal."

Her teasing was a good sign that she'd come to an understanding with herself about things. It was also often my favorite part of our time together, though it had some very stiff competition now.

I planted a solid kiss on her mouth, drawing her in for one more firm hug before pulling away. "I take care of what's mine, Grace. We have plans to make when I return."

Without waiting for a response, I left the room before I could convince myself to delay any further. I was procrastinating because this time—for the first time in ages—when I left the grounds, I was leaving behind my future.

EVEN VASSAGO COULDN'T escape the blood spatter this time.

Ophelia had been safe from the horde, thankfully, but it had been larger and more aggressive than any of the others.

Rylan had arrived to help us not long after we'd started the assault in earnest, though he didn't stay longer than a few minutes to talk once the deed was done. He flew back toward his country manor where his mate was waiting for him, still covered in gore from the fight. I was always glad to see him, and his help served to make much shorter work of our day, though we'd had the upper hand with the number of soldiers who'd turned up anyway.

A distinct impression had been made on many of the stone kin soldiers, young and old, seeing two demon princes fighting beside us. I could almost feel the shift in their viewpoints happening.

Gaius seemed even-keeled after the fight, more so than I'd seen him in recent days. We planned to talk in the next week, and I was hopeful we could come to some kind of tentative friendship after all was said and done. He mentioned quite a few points of interest about the council, and I couldn't wait to learn all the things he wanted to share.

Things were going to change soon; I felt it in the way the earth was waking up beneath my feet. I hoped we'd be together in the change and not at odds.

We left the cleaning up to the young men still in training, and flew back to d'Arcan.

"Thank you for your assistance," I said as we parted ways in the upstairs hall.

"It was my pleasure." The demon smiled. "It's been quite some time since I've done something so productive with my blade."

I barked a short laugh. Vassago was every inch the well-put-together gentleman. He might look like an angel, but I'd seen his demon out today. He'd used his fangs to tear throats out with abandon. He'd also been an absolute menace wielding a borrowed Light blade. He'd used it with such skill and confidence it might as well have been a permanent appendage.

"Well, now that I know how much fun you had, perhaps I'll invite you more often."

He bowed his head and disappeared behind his apartment door.

I cleaned myself up, growing more and more nervous. I felt like a man many years my junior as I fussed with my hair, making sure to put on the green shirt I knew Grace loved before anxiously heading back downstairs to let her know I made it back unscathed.

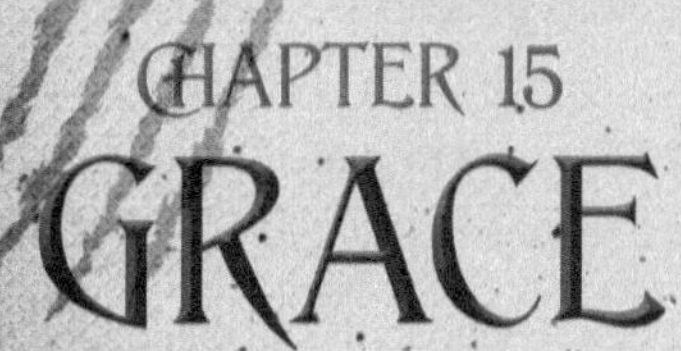

CHAPTER 15
GRACE

'D BEEN EXPECTING a knock on my apartment door for over an hour.

The pair of winged men had landed in the courtyard covered in demon gore but whole. Little Sara had let me know they were coming after leaving the dining hall after dinner. I hoped she hadn't seen more than their bodies winging their way into the yard.

I had spent the time between then and now driving myself quite mad. I'd set up a spread of food for us—him, mostly—on the little table I used for writing in my supply ledgers. I'd changed into and out of three separate dresses, only to go back to the first one again. I paced. I had conversations between the two of us all by myself and then flopped face down onto the bed.

I was not this person. This person was half my age and a fool.

Finally, the cautious tap sounded out. Patience expired, I rushed to the door and threw it open, only to immediately fling myself into the waiting gargoyle's arms.

"That's quite a welcome," he chuckled, but his arms were tight enough I knew he'd needed it too.

"You're fine?"

"Right as rain."

"Good." I let him go and invited him in. "I thought you'd be hungry."

He immediately went to one of the plates, selected a treat, and popped it in his mouth. "Always," he answered as he slid into a chair. "Join me?"

I did, but I had no appetite. I watched as he made short work of most of the things I'd brought up—which was impressive, even for him.

"Did Rylan come?"

"Yes. Vassago got quite messy, even."

"It's a miracle," I laughed. "I really was starting to wonder if that was one of his special abilities. Not getting blood on his clothing."

Magnus grunted, amused. "It is odd, right? That he never does?"

"Yes, absolutely."

He regaled me with stories from the battlefield, and my tension leaked away as he did so. I might be unfamiliar with how these things went, but I did recognize that I was comfortable with him.

"I like your apartment," he said once he'd finished his food. "It's cozier than mine."

"Smaller you mean."

He shook his head. "No, more comfortable. Your smell is everywhere, your things. The way you arrange your space gives a good insight into your mind."

"Oh? What does it say?" I was teasing, but he was more serious than I'd thought.

"That you have a heart any man would be lucky to hold, Grace."

My breath caught as he approached me, his movements slow and deliberate. He was in his human form, but never seemed to lose the ability to prowl like he did in his stone skin. Warm, broad hands held my cheeks, his brown eyes were soft as they gazed down at me.

"Can I stay with you tonight?" he asked. "I was more rested after

I slept next to you than I have been in years. Only stone sleep has left me more refreshed. But I don't want to turn to stone tonight. Not when I have a much more appealing option."

I blinked. "Of course you can." I felt silly giving my answer, but I hadn't expected the question.

"Good." He leaned down and kissed me slowly, tenderly. His lush mouth sipped at mine, little kisses that almost turned into more before he pulled away only to start again. He teased me but in the best way, making my body burn without hardly touching me at all.

He angled me toward the bed and slow steps guided me backwards until my legs hit the mattress. He lowered himself to his knees, leaning over me, still pressing those maddeningly slow, deliberate kisses onto my mouth.

Magnus used his nimble fingers to divest my body of clothing as my mind emptied thanks to his mouth. He tasted my lips, my throat, the hollow between my breasts. It seemed effortless, the way he set me on fire while worshiping me in the gentlest way possible.

When he slid off the bed to remove his own clothing, he pulled my dress the rest of the way off my body, and gestured for me to get under the blankets. "Get comfortable, Little Rabbit. Lay on your side."

I did as he asked, already damp between my legs. Magnus spooned in behind me, his cock hard and hot against my back. He adjusted my top leg forward, using his fingers to prepare me before adjusting his position and sliding into me from behind.

"We have all night, Grace. I'm going to use as much of it as I can."

He wrapped one arm around my middle, the other slipping under my pillow. He held me close as he rocked inside me, the angle creating a delicious pressure. I wrapped my free arm around his back, the two of us twined together everywhere we could manage. Magnus pressed his lips to the back of my shoulder as we clung to one another.

It was the sweetest torture when he stopped moving as my slow-building climax approached. I didn't know how much time had passed, but I whined, which only made him chuckle, and the sound rumbled low against my back.

"Soon, Little Rabbit. I just need a little longer."

He rocked into me, leisurely stroking my clit with his fingers. He moved my leg so I could experience a dozen slightly different angles, and then started all over again. Every time I got close, he stopped, leaving me a frustrated, throbbing, wet mess.

When he said he was going to take his time ... he meant it. "Please, Magnus," I begged, desperate for release.

"Patience," he growled.

I scrunched my eyes closed and tried for it, but it seemed to be him who was running out. His thrusts became more aggressive and less controlled as I spiraled into an apex thanks to the way he was pressing my legs together.

"Magnus if you deny me again, I'll disembowel you with the butter knife on that table."

"You know just the way to sweet-talk me, Grace." He panted once into my ear, and I felt his cock throb within me. I cried out as climax finally claimed me, the release intense after all the waiting, my whole body trembling. "I told you I'd take care of you," he muttered, burying his face in my shoulder.

He had. He would.

"I never doubted you." I should have been terrified by this complete upending of everything I knew, but I chose to be grateful. "I got frustrated, sure, but I never doubted." He chuckled, kissing at the skin along the curve of my shoulder.

Once I knew I could safely use my legs again, I went to clean up and stopped on my way back to drink some wine.

"Come back to bed," he muttered, nearly asleep already.

I tucked myself into his grasp again, comfortable and heavy, ready to slip off to sleep.

My heart glowed in my chest.

This was a beginning I never could have predicted, but I couldn't wait to see where it led.

Grace and Magnus's story is far from over or fully told. They will continue to appear throughout the remainder of both the Demon Princes and Gargoyle Knights series.

Not ready to say goodbye to Magnus and Grace?
Get a bonus scene by visiting:

https://BookHip.com/JRMNTWH

What's next?
Grab Book 2 of The Demon Princes Series,
The Demon's Discovery for Vassago and Greta's story!

Want to be the first to hear breaking news and other info from L.? Sign up for her newsletter!

http://bit.ly/ALANewsletter

You can also join her reader group to chat with her and other readers!

https://bit.ly/LilysReaderLounge

Did you like *The Gargoyle's Grace*? Leave a review on Amazon, Goodreads or Bookbub to share your thoughts with other readers!

ACKNOWLEDGEMENTS

This little novella was a surprise, to be honest. I didn't initially plan for Magnus to get his own book but Shain & Dannie demanded that it happen. Shain might still mad that it's so short, but I promised her Magnus and Grace will continue their story to make up for it!

Don, Shain & Dannie, you guys get so much credit for talking me through things, holding my hand and making my writing so much better, always. I heart you immeasurably.

Krista, Jessica & Stephanie always put up with my shenanigans trying to get things clean and pretty! I couldn't do it without your help and I mean that.

Meri, you get a special THANKS because you waited the longest to see everyone else get their hands on this one. Haha XOXO

ARC readers! Do you even know how vital you are to authors like me? I hope you do. You're the cat's freaking pajamas and I cannot express how grateful I am to you! Seeing any post with my stuff on it is a humbling, thrilling experience. I couldn't do this without you.

I can't wait for you all to see what's coming next! There are more demons to make fall in love, and some stone kin I can't wait to help find their mates.

Note: This world is planned to be seven books, one for each brother PLUS a novella for our stone kin friends in-between. I hope you stick with us!

For sneak peeks, discussion and other fun tidbits, make sure you're signed up for my newsletter, & join my reader group.

ABOUT THE AUTHOR

L. Alexander writes Paranormal and Fantasy romance with sweet & spicy cinnamon roll heroes, fated mates, monsters, magic and more. She guarantees a happily ever after no matter what and has a soft spot for broody anime characters.

www.authorlilyalexander.com

@lilyalexanderwrites on Instagram

Lily Alexander on Facebook, TikTok, BookBub and Goodreads

L. also writes Contemporary Romance under the name Lily Alexander.

www.ingramcontent.com/pod-product-compliance
Lightning Source LLC
Chambersburg PA
CBHW031057310726
48969CB00007B/2322